BURNING ELVIS

John Burnside was born in 1955 and now lives in Fife. He has published seven collections of poetry and has won a number of awards, including the Geoffrey Faber Memorial Prize. He was selected as one of the twenty Best of Young British Poets in 1994. He has published two novels, *The Dumb House* (1997) and *The Mercy Boys* (1999).

D0785984

BURNING ELVIS

JOHN BURNSIDE

Jonathan Cape
London

Published by Jonathan Cape 2000

2 4 6 8 10 9 7 5 3 1

First published in Great Britain in 2000 by
Jonathan Cape
Random House, 20 Vauxhall Bridge Road,
London SW1V 2SA

Random House Australia (Pty) Limited
20 Alfred Street, Milsons Point, Sydney,
New South Wales 2061, Australia

Random House New Zealand Limited
18 Poland Road, Glenfield,
Auckland 10, New Zealand

Random House South Africa (Pty) Limited
Endulini, 5A Jubilee Road, Parktown 2193, South Africa

The Random House Group Limited Reg. No. 954009
www.randomhouse.co.uk

A CIP catalogue record for this book
is available from the British Library

ISBN 0 224 05008 7

Papers used by Random House are natural,
recyclable products made from wood grown in sustainable forests;
the manufacturing processes conform to the environmental
regulations of the country of origin

Typeset by Palimpsest Book Production Limited,
Polmont, Stirlingshire
Printed and bound in Great Britain by
Biddles Ltd, Guildford and King's Lynn

for my sisters

Quhat have we here bot grace us to defend?

Robert Henryson

Contents

Acknowledgments are due to BBC Radio 4, *The Ex-Files*, *New Writing 6*, *NeonLit*, *Soho Square VII*, and *Southfields*.

BURNING ELVIS

No man is an island.

John Donne

I don't know why I choose to remember one thing, rather than another. Maybe whatever it was that happened turned out to be the myth I needed – the myth, or the necessary lie, which comes to the same thing: it's a Tuesday afternoon, early in the summer; it's already too hot and I've come indoors, into the shade. Idly, I switch on the television and start watching a documentary, something about America in the early sixties: JFK, the space program, the sad innocence of consumerism. It doesn't capture my attention, it's just background for a while – I even go out to the kitchen halfway through and pour myself a long, cold drink. I fill the glass with ice and mint leaves and carry it back, almost unbearably aware of myself as an isolated body in a closed space – and that's when I see her: a young girl in a light-brown uniform, with a scarlet cap, in a sun-bleached garden somewhere in Texas or Arkansas: a dark-haired girl with a bob, dancing, or playing hopscotch, half-aware of the camera. She's smiling – to herself, mostly – and she seems happy. It's not that she looks so much like Lindy; or if she does, the resemblance is superficial. It's just that smile, that sense of herself as a complicated game, and maybe it's the faded sunlight, the suggestion of a life beyond the film, a long childhood of beaches and Christmas trees that never really happened. When the programme ends, I stand looking out at the empty street: the suburb on a weekday afternoon, clipped lawns

3

and pools of shadow, an astonishing stillness, that moment's sense of being alone, of turning around and finding the whole thing – the whole world – is a calculated illusion.

It was spring when the Andersons moved in next door. I first saw Lindy one afternoon, out beyond the fence, where the houses back on to the old nurseries. I used to go wandering out there to escape Mother's neatly manicured garden. You could still see the odd clump of irises, the rows of shrubs laced with bindweed, but mostly it was derelict and overgrown, with wide milky puddles in winter, and lush docks and nightshades in the summertime. I liked it there, I liked the way it had been reclaimed by wildness: the sheds collapsing slowly under the weeds and the rain; the tarmac cracking, shot with mayweed, the hedges blurring, everything running to seed. I didn't notice Lindy to begin with, but I knew someone was there. It was only when I climbed the bank and looked down that I saw her, sitting among the hogweed and nettles, smoking a cigarette. She looked up into the sunlight: a thin, lithe girl with short black hair, who seemed, in that first moment, almost unbelievably beautiful. She looked at me curiously, as if I was some strange animal she had met out there among the bushes and briars. There was a brightness in her eyes, a look of expectation that made me expect something too, but she didn't speak, she didn't even acknowledge my presence, she just took a long drag on her cigarette and looked away.

'I suppose you're the kid from next door,' she said at last.

I laughed. It was funny, her calling me a kid, when I was older.

'Do you go to Saint Mary's?' she asked and, though I didn't know her, I could tell she was being somebody else, a character in a film she'd seen, cool and distant, one of the untouchables. I nodded.

'I'm in the fifth year,' I said, pointedly.

She smiled.

'So what's it like?'

I shrugged.

'It's all right.'

She stood up and smoothed her dress.

'Well, I don't suppose it matters. One school's much like another.' She looked me up and down, as if she was trying to memorise my appearance, then she smiled sweetly, and climbed to the top of the bank.

'You didn't see the cigarette,' she said; then she gave me an odd wave, and walked back towards the houses.

She must have started school the next morning. I didn't see her for a couple of days, then I met her on the street, walking home, and we started to talk. I still remember everything she said that first day, and on the days that followed. I remember everything she did, every move she made, the clothes she wore, the way she kept flicking her hair out of her eyes. After that, I started to hang around outside school, so I could casually walk her home, and we fell into a game, where she didn't notice that I had waited, and I pretended I'd met her by accident, outside the gates, or fifty yards along the road. Sometimes we'd stand outside her house and talk for hours. I used to wonder what her parents thought, but I needn't have worried: Lindy got to do pretty much what she wanted. Once, when it began to rain, she called out to me, as I walked away, that I should come inside next time. I remember clearly, even now, the absurd happiness I felt.

Lindy was thirteen. She was two years behind me at school, but she seemed older. She liked old Hollywood films, especially horror movies. She knew who directed what, and when; she knew the names and biographies of the actors. Her particular favourite was Gloria Holden, in the 1936 film *Dracula's Daughter*. She'd talk about that picture for hours: the mysterious woman's desperate longing to be released from her dark nature, the way she would tilt her head to listen through the soundtrack for something she alone could hear, and that moment when she surrendered – the self-mocking smile, the fuzz of blood on her teeth, the slow glide to meet her next victim. Once I got to know her a little, it didn't surprise me that she liked that stuff. She liked to make a mystery of things. I sometimes had the impression she'd been thinking for years about questions nobody else even considered, and she'd moved away, into a parallel life, with its own incontrovertible logic. Half the time, I didn't understand a word she was saying. She pretended to know about science: she'd talk about microfossils, cosmic dust, theories of evolution. Sometimes I guessed she was making it up as she went along, but I'd be impressed anyway. Everything she said lodged in my mind, as if it were indisputable fact. Even now, things surface from time to time, and I realise it's all there, mingled with the memorised hymns, with Boyle's Law and the basics of topology, part of the seamless fabric of my schooldays, gathered up and put away, like one of those huge crazy-quilts my mother used to make from scraps of left-over material.

We would meet at weekends, in the nursery grounds, out by the old potting sheds. It was damp out there, in the shade; you could smell peat and mildew, and something else beyond the currant bushes and the viburnums, a dark, fenny smell, touched with spawn and duckweed – something ancient, almost primeval, lurking in the remnants of orange boxes and peat bags beyond the rotting doors. We'd sit there on Saturday afternoons, suspended in time, separated from the rest of the world by a fine membrane of must and warmth. Mostly, she would talk and I would listen. Sometimes we argued about films or music. She'd tell me I was a snob, because I didn't like Hollywood: she said art films were good, but that wasn't why I liked them – she said I liked them because they were art films. She used to annoy me some of the time, to be honest. But most of the time, she would talk about things that bothered her, like who killed Kennedy, or what really happened to Marilyn Monroe. One day she started talking about Elvis, about how every fault was magnified in him because, for a short time, he had been perfect. It might not have mattered, if nobody had witnessed this perfection, but they had, and it had become a historical fact. She said the story of Elvis's life was like any other myth where the hero comes into being. Perfection can happen, but it can't last, because people don't want it to last. They want a crucifixion; they want the phoenix. They want the idea but they don't want the person. If Elvis had died before he went into films, they would have loved him for ever and unconditionally. But he didn't die. He lived and his perfection was corrupted. Whatever he did that wasn't perfect was seized upon with relish and disbelief by people who had never loved him anyway. She said fans didn't love their heroes, they just consumed them. She said anyone who had really loved Elvis would have helped him, by making him see that he was the phoenix, and he had to be burned. People think the phoenix story is about how everything that dies is reborn from its own ashes, but Lindy thought the real meaning was in the flames, not the ashes, not the rebirth, but the necessary burning.

I listened, but I didn't really understand what she meant. Elvis barely existed for me: I remembered seeing his films at matinees, when I was a kid; I had a vague recollection of contained grace, and a kind of beauty that seemed remote and aimless, like the beauty of the tigers at the zoo. I knew he'd died a couple of years before, but I couldn't remember when.

'There are people who think he's still alive,' she said.

'That always happens,' I told her. 'They said the same thing about James Dean.'

She gave me a disdainful look and shook her head.

'Elvis is different,' she said.

I didn't see how, but I didn't want to argue. When it came to stuff like that, Lindy knew what she knew; she had her own system of beliefs and theories that were too beautiful to doubt.

'He should never have gone into films,' she continued. 'John Lennon said Elvis died when he went into the army, but I don't think that's true. It was the films.'

She lit a cigarette and stared off into space. I already knew that look: the rapt gaze of someone who lived entirely in her own world, utterly self-contained, and quite unattainable, and I believe, even then, that I had a sense of what was going to happen. Maybe this is hindsight, but I don't think so. It was subtle, and I couldn't have pointed to any one thing, but something about her made me suspect a complicity with what happened later. It was the way she smoked, the way she talked, the way she was never still, never at rest.

'What we have to do,' she said after a while, 'is redeem Elvis.'

I laughed.

'And how are you going to do that?' I asked.

'By fire, of course.' She turned to me and smiled. 'Do you have a camera?'

'Yes.'

'Come round to my house next Saturday. Bring the camera. I'll tell you about it then.'

'Tell me now.'

She stubbed out her half-smoked cigarette and shook her head.

'Wait,' she said.

The following Saturday I went over to her house at ten o'clock in the morning. It was a changeable day, but the light was good. I'd bought a new film, and cleaned the camera. It was an expensive 35mm SLR that Dad had given me the previous Christmas.

Mrs Anderson opened the door.

'Lindy's expecting you,' she said. 'Go on up. It's the first on the left.'

Her room was a mess. The floor was littered with sequins and beads, battered toys, pieces of clockwork, dolls' heads, old apothecary's bottles marked *Poison* or *Acid*. There was a pin-board above the bed, covered with photographs and stills of old-time Hollywood actresses: Hedy Lamarr, Joan Fontaine, Louise Brooks, Gloria Holden. The only picture that wasn't a still from a film was the famous Vietnam shot, the one Eddie Adams took of a South Vietnamese general shooting a prisoner in the head. It was a page she'd torn from a magazine: the prisoner, a thin man in a check shirt, has his hands tied behind his back, and his face is twisted with fear; though he isn't looking directly at the gun, he knows how close it is. I heard later that the picture was taken at the moment the weapon was fired, at the very moment the bullet entered his head.

The other wall was covered with drawings that she'd tacked up casually with a strip of sellotape; some were rough sketches, others were finely detailed, but they were all beautifully executed. They were also bizarre. A few showed scenes from old horror movies, but most were drawings of Elvis. The one I remember best showed him in his prime, in a black leather jacket, a sneer on his lips, his hair unruly. The face was beautiful, alive, arrogant – but under the jacket there was no body, only a set of ribs and a spine, and a white pelvis fading away into nothingness at the edge of the page. It's hard to describe – it sounds like the morbid imaginings of a teenage girl but for me there was more, a surprising poignancy, a glimpse of vacuum. Lindy told me she'd made that drawing on the night Elvis died.

The effigy was sitting in an old leather armchair, next to her desk, dressed in a cream-coloured jacket and black jeans. I didn't know then who it was, of course: the head was a blank – no face, no hair, just an old sack crammed with straw. Except for the clothes, the figure she'd made looked more like a guy for Bonfire Night than anything else.

'What's this?' I asked.

Lindy smiled mysteriously and went to the bedside table. She took something out of a drawer and walked over to the dummy, keeping her back to me, so I couldn't see what she was doing.

'Finished,' she said.

The dummy had become Elvis. It was wearing one of those masks you could buy from joke shops, the kind that covered your whole head, and just had pinholes for the mouth and eyes. It looked quite realistic, I suppose, for a piece of moulded rubber.

'It's not that great,' Lindy said. 'But it doesn't matter. By the time we're taking the pictures, it'll look like real.'

I nodded, but I wasn't convinced. As far as I could see, it was as good a likeness as it was going to get.

Lindy's mother went shopping around eleven. We waited till she had gone, then we hauled the effigy through the house and out the back door. Or rather, I did. Lindy carried the camera. On the way, she ducked into the shed at the end of her garden, and emerged carrying a large red petrol can.

'We'll need this,' she said.

As we walked, she explained the plan. We would take Elvis over to the potting sheds, where no one would see. Lindy had found a stake out there, which we would use to support the effigy while it burned. When it caught fire, I had to start taking pictures, and I couldn't stop till she told me. I was pretty nervous. If somebody came, it would be difficult to explain what we were doing. They might think we were starting a real fire. Needless to say, I did all the carrying. Lindy walked on, a few paces ahead, talking non-stop, to keep me distracted, so I wouldn't chicken out.

'Did you know Elvis had a twin brother?'

I didn't answer. I was holding the effigy round the waist, so the mask was a few inches from my face; every time I took a step, the legs banged against my knees and I had to keep stopping to get a better grip.

'It's true. His name was Jesse Garon. He was stillborn, I think. Or maybe he died soon after he was born. Elvis's father put him in a shoebox and buried him in an unmarked grave, somewhere in the woods in Tennessee.'

She kept talking till we reached the potting sheds, then she found the stake and pushed it into the ground. She pulled some twine out of her jacket pocket and I helped her tie the effigy to the stake, so it was almost upright. The top half of the body slumped to one side, and she fussed with it for a while, till she got it straight. It didn't look much like Elvis to me; it didn't look like a person at all. Lindy had tucked the top of the mask into the collar of the jacket, but there was still a brown patch where the sacking showed through, and there was something less than life-size about the figure, a slackness that reminded me again of the guy at a bonfire. Still, Lindy seemed happy enough.

'Is the camera ready?' she asked.

11

I wound on the film and offered it to her, but she shook her head.

'It's your camera,' she said. 'You do it.'

She took a good look round and, when she was certain nobody had seen us, she splashed the effigy with petrol. For a moment it shivered, as if it was about to fall, then it burst into flames as Lindy tossed a match and leapt out of the way.

'Go,' she shouted.

I started taking the pictures. Seen through the lens, the burning figure looked more real, more like a person. Amid the smoke and flames, the mask became a face, and I moved in closer, as the body twisted and crumpled, trying to catch the image of burning flesh that was almost visible for a moment, before the material blistered and fizzled away. It was incredible. It couldn't have lasted more than a minute or two, but I really believed I had caught a glimpse of the real Elvis, the Hillbilly Cat, the Elvis Lindy wanted me to see.

'All right,' she said, as the body fell and started to burn out. 'We've got enough pictures.'

I turned and looked at her. My face was hot and flushed from the heat of the fire, and I felt exhilarated. All of a sudden, I understood what we were doing. I understood everything. I looked up: small white clouds were drifting across the sky, but right above my head there was a gap, a patch of deep, mineral blue, like the colour of lapis lazuli when it is moistened and warmed by the breath. I felt dizzy. At that moment, there was no way of distinguishing between me and Lindy and this patch of sky. Everything was seamless. I looked at her.

'This is amazing,' I said.

She shook her head and smiled sadly.

'Let's have a cigarette,' she said.

★   ★   ★

Memory is something mineral, a deposit that builds up over years. It has nothing to do with the past; it's entirely a matter of what is wanted in the present. Yet I'd like to believe, in some objective way, that that was the happiest summer of my life. Burning Elvis had created a complicity between us; I felt we had shared something, that we were similar, bound by a common spirit. I started smoking, to keep her company. We would meet by the sheds: Lindy would bring a packet of Sovereigns, and we would lie on our backs, staring up at the sky, smoking and talking. I suppose I'd begun to think of her as my girlfriend, though neither of us had ever said or done anything to justify the assumption. I wanted to touch her; I wanted to kiss her face; I wanted to unbutton her blouse and stroke my finger lightly along the ridge of her collar bone. She would wear a short blue skirt with white polka dots. Her legs were golden; her thighs and arms were covered with a soft silvery-blonde down that I ached to touch. But I never did. Maybe I knew she would refuse me: the only way I could keep alive my fantasy that we were virtual lovers was to stay behind an invisible line that she had somehow drawn between us, without a word or a gesture that I could recall.

One afternoon, towards the end of the holidays, we were out on the other side of the field, sitting in the lowest branches of a spreading maple tree. There was a pause in the conversation and I looked at her. It was the one time I came close to crossing the line, and Lindy must have read my mind, because she slipped to the ground suddenly, and looked up at me.

'Do you know Kiwi Johnson?' she said.

'Who?'

'Kiwi,' she repeated. 'Kiwi Johnson.'

I nodded slowly. I remembered Kiwi Johnson all right: he'd been in the fifth year when I was in lower school, and I didn't like him. Nobody did. He was one of those boys you see in the corner of any playground, pretending he isn't there. I could tell, just by looking at him, that he thought he was different from the others. He wasn't excluded, he just didn't want to join in. In games lessons, when the captains were choosing teams, he was always one of the last to be picked, not because he wasn't any good, but because he resisted selection. Whenever a team captain looked in his direction, he would stare back coldly, as if he was daring the boy to choose him, and the captain would move on, taking Pig Lee, or Specky Aldrick, rather than face that malevolent gaze. It made people resent him. Usually, if a boy was picked towards the end, because he was fat or effeminate, or generally despised for no good reason, he would run into line quickly, grateful to be chosen at all. Those boys were always on the alert, ready to accept without protest their apportioned share of humiliation. They knew they were despised: they were always fussing, trying to appease everyone at once, making silent promises with their eyes, to try harder, to be what was wanted. Kiwi Johnson stood apart from all that. He made it clear that he didn't want to join in – if it hadn't been for the teacher, he wouldn't even have bothered. Yet when he was forced to take part, he played with a cold, deliberate brutality that surprised everyone. It was a kind of challenge. In one football game, Mr Williams made him play forward, instead of his usual position, at left back. About halfway through the period, someone accidentally passed him the ball directly in front of the net: he paused a moment, looked at the opposing goalkeeper, a small, wiry boy called Manny Doyle, then he punted the ball straight at his head. It was a cold, wet day. Our year was out on the other field, about a hundred yards away, but we all saw Manny go down. Later, he said it was mostly his fault – he'd seen the ball coming, he just hadn't ducked in time. Kiwi didn't say anything, he only glanced round at Mr Williams, as if to say, *now look what you've made me do.*

I used to wonder how he got the name Kiwi. It wasn't a nickname: there was no affection in it. There was no real venom either, but it was still an expression of dislike, like some of the names we gave to teachers, and nobody used it to his face. Once, Des Coffey followed him around the playground, taunting him, and they were obliged to fight. People who remember nothing else from school can still picture that December afternoon, the week before the holidays. In those days, we had rules; there was an underlying code that prevented anyone going too far, so the damage was always more imagined than real. But this was one of those occasions when the rules might not hold, and everybody was excited. Nobody had ever seen Kiwi in a fight before, but most of us thought Des would win. He was in Kiwi's year, but he was much bigger, and a famous dirty fighter.

The two boys met outside the gates and fought for fifteen minutes in a drift of falling snow. Usually, when a fight happened, there would be gangs of followers egging their boy on, urging him to acts of viciousness that were never serious possibilities – *smash his face, kick his teeth in,* that kind of thing. But this fight was conducted in total silence. We just stood there, awed, as we watched the first real battering we had ever witnessed. When it was over, Kiwi walked away with a handkerchief pressed to his mouth, but Des Coffey had been punched and kicked so systematically, he was almost unrecognisable. Quite a few of the spectators were friends of his, but nobody lifted a finger to stop the punishment. That was another part of the code. Everybody knew it was stupid, but nobody questioned it. If you called somebody out for a fight, you accepted the consequences.

Now Kiwi would be nineteen, maybe twenty. He'd left

school at the end of the fifth year and as far as I knew he was working at Scandex, making gaskets. I'd seen him in town, on a motor-bike: he wore a cutaway Levi's jacket and had lurid tattoos on his hands. He'd been in trouble a couple of times, but I couldn't remember why. Now, I looked at Lindy in amazement.

'Kiwi Johnson?' I said, with obvious distaste.

She laughed.

'Have you seen his tattoos?'

I was annoyed now. I didn't know what bothered me most, that she would be interested in someone like Kiwi, or that she would tell *me* about it, as if I was some girl friend from school.

'I think he goes out with Cathy Gillespie,' I said.

'Well he used to,' Lindy said, looking pleased with herself.

I dropped out of the tree and stood facing her.

'And?'

She laughed again.

'And what?'

'Why are you so interested in Kiwi Johnson?' I said, realising I sounded like the jealous boyfriend I wasn't.

'Why shouldn't I be?' Lindy answered coolly. 'He's interesting.'

I felt sick. As far as I was concerned, Kiwi Johnson looked like one of the bad guys that Elvis was always beating up in his films. I started to walk away, thinking Lindy would call me back, and tell me it was all a joke – she didn't like Kiwi at all, she was just pulling my leg to see what I would do. But she didn't. I got as far as the bank before I stopped and looked round. Lindy was standing under the tree, lighting a cigarette. As far as I could tell, she had already forgotten I existed.

That was the end of an idyll. As I remember it now, I still saw Lindy every day, but she was remote from me, neutral, preoccupied with something. I had no doubt she was thinking about Kiwi; I didn't think she was going out with him. But towards the end of the holidays, I learned different. I'd met Lindy in town: as always, whenever I was with her, I was totally absorbed, the rest of the world might not have existed for all I cared, and I didn't know anybody was there until, with an odd, almost imperceptible shift, I felt Lindy detach herself from me. I turned and saw Kiwi and another bloke, a tall thin guy with straggly henna-coloured hair; the two of them were listening with mock-seriousness to whatever it was I had been saying. A moment before, Lindy had been with me, now she was with them, and there was a gap between us. I was the outsider, and Kiwi knew it. He took Lindy's arm.

'We're going over to Dave's place,' he said. 'Do you want to come?'

'OK,' Lindy said. She didn't make any move to free herself, to make him let go of her, and I realised it wasn't the first time he had touched her. I was disgusted and fascinated. In all the time I'd known Lindy, I'd never touched her, not even accidentally. There was a kind of unwritten law about it, a zone around her body that nobody was supposed to enter.

Kiwi glanced at me and Lindy turned guiltily. I knew she would have left me there, if he hadn't intervened.

'How about you?' he asked.

'I don't know,' I answered. I didn't want to leave Lindy with them, but I didn't want to go to Dave's place either.

'You ought to come, too,' Kiwi said. 'You should take a look at Dave's pictures. Did you know Dave was a painter?'

I looked at Dave, helplessly. There was no way out, without looking like an idiot, or a coward. Dave grinned, and we went to his place.

★   ★   ★

17

I only remember the first part of that afternoon. Kiwi offered to read Lindy's palm, while Dave took me into another room to show me his pictures. As I remember them now, I have to admit they were very good, in spite of the subject matter. Dave showed me the book he'd used as a source for most of them – some specialist text on crime-scene forensics, with full-colour plates showing murder victims in a variety of poses: a woman tied and gagged, with her throat cut open; a man with his face shot away; what looked like a teenage girl, with one leg cut off just below the knee, and both hands cleanly amputated, the look on her face a mask of unimaginable horror. The paintings were huge: the stylised figures they portrayed were obviously drawn from the photographs in the textbook, but they had been subtly altered. All the pain had been leached away and what remained was like the end of a game, or a ritual: the figures were not so much victims as icons.

I looked at Dave.

'Don't say anything,' he said. 'I don't want you to make any comment. All right?'

When we got back, Kiwi was studying Lindy's hands as if he really understood what he was doing. Of course, I knew it was a sham: he was aware of me all the time, he could see it annoyed me that he was touching her, that he could so easily form an intimacy with her from which I was excluded. Lindy was joining in; she seemed to take him seriously, attentive to everything he said, murmuring agreement from time to time, elucidating, confirming, asking questions. It offended me that she could believe the lines in her hand contained some arcane text that only he could read. It didn't matter that it was all an act, what mattered was the complicity between them, the way she allowed him to elicit memories and confessions with his carefully open-ended remarks: a history she hadn't thought to share with me, she offered casually to him, because he was special, he was the gifted one.

Dave made some coffee. When Kiwi had finished with Lindy's palm, he offered to read mine, knowing I wouldn't agree. I felt my refusal was taken as an evasion, as if I were afraid he would discover a secret I preferred to keep hidden, something I would be ashamed of in front of Lindy. I remember wanting to leave and not knowing how; then, before I really knew what was happening, Dave took something out of a box and started cutting it up with a razor. He kept looking at me and smiling, then he put something in his mouth, and handed each of us a tiny particle of what looked like dirt. I watched Kiwi take his piece and put it on his tongue, then Lindy did the same. They were all looking at me, smiling, almost friendly, waiting to see what I would do. I put the grain of dirt in my mouth, and let it dissolve. Lindy smiled and kicked off her shoes.

I didn't feel any effects for about half an hour. Dave put on some music and started talking to me, but I wasn't really listening. I heard Kiwi say to Lindy that he liked the pictures: at first I didn't know what pictures he meant, but then they started talking about Elvis and I realised she'd given him the photographs I'd taken at the burning. I was angry. Dave was talking about the Nazis: he started showing me pictures of young women from some Hitler youth organisation: they were performing gymnastics or playing games with hula-hoops, all tall and slender and unimpeachably Aryan. Dave told me how he'd seen films of these women when he was a kid and he'd been obsessed with them ever since. I was trying to hear what the others were saying – they seemed to be arguing about Elvis's father, arguing and laughing, touching one another from time to time, exploring, entering and retreating, establishing something.

19

On the other side of the room, they suddenly seemed far away; Dave kept talking, flicking through the book and confessing to me how these were the only women he liked, these blonde Hitler girls in their white shifts. I couldn't tell if he was being serious.

After a while, my body began to feel warm and a little tight, as if my skin had been stretched, like the surface of a drum. I remember a moment's panic, the thought that something would snap, like a piece of catgut, then I let go and relaxed. Time had slipped. I was alone in the room now, but I could hear voices. They were close to my face, only inches away, whispering softly, almost unbearably kind, all the people in Dave's paintings, whispering through great pain, merging one into another, into a single, multi-threaded voice.

'*Come home now.*'

'*Listen.*'

'*You know where you are.*'

'*Come in. Come in.*'

'*Listen.*'

Then another voice came through the haze, much clearer, a voice I recognised but couldn't put a name to.

'I'm waiting for you,' it said. 'I won't let you fall.' Then I saw Dave, sitting on the edge of the bed.

'Are you OK?' he asked.

I nodded.

He reached out to stroke my face, and I drew back in alarm.

'Where's Lindy?' I almost shouted. It didn't sound like my voice, it sounded like one of those others, one of those people in the paintings.

Dave bent down and kissed me on the forehead. I stiffened and lay still, with my arms at my side.

'Don't worry, baby,' he said. 'Take it easy.'

He laughed softly.

'There will always be a father.'

I caught a trace of the smell as soon as I opened the door. It was stronger in the hall than it was in the porch: a smell of damp clothes, an old coat, or a jacket, saturated with dirt and rain. I thought someone had broken in, and I hesitated – what if he was still there, in the dining room, or somewhere upstairs, startled by the sound of my key in the door, standing still, holding his breath, waiting to hear what I'd do next. I listened. It was a long time before I dared to push open the dining room door and look inside: the smell was even stronger now, and I couldn't understand it – it was definitely the smell of stale, wet clothes, but how could the intruder be wet, when it wasn't raining outside, when it hadn't rained for days? I walked through to the kitchen. The back door was open and there, on the threshold, I saw a naked footprint, just one, dark and perfectly defined on the light cement. I froze. I knew who it was who had been there. I don't know how, but I did, and I wasn't afraid: I felt as if I'd just received a secret message, or a sign, and it had something to do with the drug Dave had given me. It was a riddle that I'd been set: now, all of a sudden, I knew how to solve it. I slipped off my shoe and placed my foot over the print. It was a perfect fit, just as I'd expected. I smiled then, and shook my head. It didn't matter now that everything was out of focus. It didn't even matter about Kiwi. I was happy; I understood everything; it was my life that was happening, nobody else's. I walked across the garden and climbed the fence into the nursery grounds. I was certain he was out there, hidden among the shrubs, crouched in the long grass, waiting for me. It was hours before I gave up the search.

★   ★   ★

21

I didn't see Lindy till after term started. I felt bad: I couldn't remember where she'd gone that afternoon at Dave's flat. I couldn't even remember how I'd got home. That day had ripped a hole in my life, in everything I took for granted. I pretended to my parents that I had a summer cold and stayed in bed for a couple of days, to try and collect my thoughts. Then, even when I did see Lindy, I didn't know what to say to her. I had convinced myself that she was part of some plan to humiliate me. I thought she had worked the whole thing out with Kiwi and Dave: the drugs, the voices, even the phantom footprint. It was all her fault.

For her part, she hardly seemed to notice me. She existed in her own space, and I began to understand that I'd never had anything more than a marginal place there. I used to imagine that knowledge was the beginning of change, but I suppose I've always known that there was too little between me and the rest of the world, that I'm all surface, all availability, and I haven't been able to change that. I'm still the same as I was that day, when Dave and Kiwi showed me how remote I was from the centre of Lindy's world. Looking back, I understand now how unaccountably gentle they were, how what I took for a cruel trick on Dave's part was really a bizarre form of courtesy. He wanted me to see that I was different in kind from people like Lindy and Kiwi, that they were fearless in a way I could never be. I was too attached to myself, I wanted to understand too much, to always know where I was. He was letting me know that it was all right, that there was nothing I could do about it, but at the time I only felt ashamed, as if I'd discovered a flaw in my soul, a weakness I would never overcome.

A couple of weeks later, we were playing *Judex* at the school film club. It was the first show of the new academic year and I was involved in organising the event. As a conciliatory gesture, I caught up with Lindy on the way home and asked her if she wanted to come, but she just looked mysterious and told me she had something else on.

'Really?' I said, trying to sound casual. 'Anything interesting?'

'I'm going out.'

'On your own?'

She paused, partly for effect, partly because she hadn't decided if she wanted to tell me.

'Well, not that it's any of your business,' she said. 'But I'm going out with Kiwi. On his bike.'

I'd suspected that, but I must have looked hurt nevertheless. Lindy shook her head.

'Don't be a drag,' she said. 'It's just a bike ride. Anyway, you don't know what he's like.'

'And you do I suppose?' I was more irritated than I had meant to sound.

'Yes.'

She stared at me with that sublime assurance of hers, and I knew it was too late to change her mind.

'I like him,' she said.

I didn't speak. By now I was wondering how far it had gone. I had a sickening flash of Kiwi's hands, with their blue and scarlet tattoos, poised at the hem of Lindy's dress. I even had an ugly, fleeting idea of them together, and Dave watching, in that room of his, filled with pictures of the dead. I turned away, so I wouldn't have to look at her.

'God,' she said. 'You don't understand anything.'

I looked back at her. I wanted to sound neutral, with a hint of older and wiser, but it didn't come out that way. Even to myself, I sounded petty.

'I just don't trust Kiwi Johnson,' I said. 'And if you had any sense, you wouldn't either.'

She shook her head again. She seemed sad.

'I can look after myself,' she said quietly. 'Don't worry about me.'

'I won't,' I answered. I was ashamed of myself as soon as I said it, but it was too late by then. Lindy walked quickly to her door and let herself in without looking back, and I just stood there, watching her go, telling myself I didn't care anyway, sick to the stomach with jealousy and self-disgust.

I didn't go to the film club. It was a windy night, with occasional gusts of rain blowing through the cypress hedges and rustling against the windows like fine sand. Dad was away, and Mother was upstairs, locked in the secret room of a migraine. Whenever she got one of those attacks she was distant and silent, as if she wanted to reduce her presence in the world to an absolute minimum.

I was restless. It sounds like the wisdom of hindsight, but I really did believe something bad would happen. I had a book open on the table, but I couldn't read. I kept glancing up at the circle of streetlight outside our gate and the darkness beyond, at the small white blur of the Andersons' porch lamp, and the privet hedges glistening under the fine rain. I didn't see anyone. Later I asked myself a hundred times where Cathy was all that time. She must have been waiting somewhere for Lindy to come home. She might have been standing outside our house for hours, hidden in the shadows, but in all that time, I didn't see her. Kiwi dropped Lindy at the end of the street, so her parents wouldn't know who she was with. It turned out later that they thought she was over at my house. She'd walked into the circle of lamplight outside our door, and Cathy had met her, silently, bringing the knife up out of the shadows. It must have happened while I turned a page or glanced at the clock – by the time I knew anything about it, it was over. It was a quarter past eleven. Somebody made a sound – not so much a scream as a half-finished cry – but I didn't recognise the voice as belonging to Lindy. I looked out of the window and I saw Cathy Gillespie under the streetlamp, just outside our gate. She was looking at something on the ground.

I ran out. Lindy was lying face-down on the pavement. She was still moving – I think she was trying to get up – and she was making a low, gurgling sound in her throat, as if she was choking on something. Cathy had stabbed her in the neck: there was blood everywhere, on the hedges, on Cathy's clothes, all over the pavement. I couldn't move. Cathy was standing beside me, holding the knife, but I made no attempt to get it off her, or to help Lindy. I think I already understood it was too late.

The night was still warm, in spite of the rain. The privet was in flower and I caught the faint, vanilla taste of it through the smell of the blood. It bothers me now, that I can remember it all so clearly – to think that I was so aware of everything, yet still failed to act. I should have run back indoors and called for an ambulance. I should have tried to give her the kiss of life. I suppose I was in shock, but I still knew Lindy was dying. I remember thinking it: there was something about her body – she seemed smaller than before, less substantial, as if some essence had already begun to drain away.

I don't know how long it was before I heard the siren. That was the first time I became aware of the voices; someone had his hand on my shoulder and was telling me to go back inside. I turned and saw Mr Carpenter, from across the street. Someone else was holding Cathy by the arm: it was a man I didn't really know, who lived a few doors away. Cathy had dropped the knife, or someone had knocked it out of her hand – it had a long, pointed blade, and a black handle. She had probably stolen it from her parents' kitchen. The man who was holding her was wearing a dressing gown and a pair of grey woollen slippers. In the light from the streetlamp, I could see that the slippers were splashed with Lindy's blood.

I saw Cathy in the town centre three weeks after she got home. It was about four in the afternoon: she was standing in the market square on her own, smoking a cigarette; she looked nervous and lonely, and I caught myself feeling sorry for her. She had the look of someone who's come back to a place and found it changed beyond recognition, inhabited by strangers who don't even speak her language or live their lives by the same landmarks that she once knew. She was looking at the people passing by: she paid special attention to the school kids gathering at the bus station – it was as if she had forgotten that seven years had passed, and all her old friends were grown up now, with kids of their own and jobs at Smiths or Scandex.

I stopped and watched her for a while. She didn't notice me – or if she did, I was as much a stranger to her as the other people in the square. Or not a stranger so much as a phantom. It was some time before I realised she was waiting for someone, and I went on about my business. She must have been stood up, because she was still there, in the gathering twilight, when I came by later, with my bag of groceries and an armful of library books. I was pretty sure that, whoever she'd been waiting for, it was somebody who knew her from the old days. Nobody else knew who she was and I think that frightened her, as if the whole thing had been a dream, or the story of something that hadn't really happened. I wondered if she understood the futility of her actions. In all her life – in my life, too – it was the one defining event, the moment that stood out, and it could

never be repeated. Now we were folding back into time: Lindy
was dead, Kiwi had gone off somewhere, and she was standing
there, smoking another cigarette, waiting for someone to turn
up and make it all real. I suppose I could have performed that
office; I could have walked over and spoken to her. Just to
say her name would have been enough: she wouldn't have to
recognise me. All she needed was for someone to remember –
it would be like that moment when Dracula's daughter passes
the empty mirror and the audience sees who she is. The worst
thing about a secret is to be forced to keep it for ever. People
will kill for the sensation of being, just to see themselves in the
story. Lindy used to say that everybody wants to be special; but
Cathy wasn't special at all, she was nothing. Her fragment of
history had passed and nobody knew or cared who she was.
Life had moved on. It was a banal and surprisingly comforting
thought, and all of a sudden it made me unaccountably glad, like
the stillness of a city graveyard, or the first thick fall of snow, that
obliterates and renews everything it touches.

WHAT I KNOW ABOUT MYSELF

He's a peninsula.

Jefferson Airplane

My father used to tell me I wasn't his son. He had several explanations for my presence in his house: I was a foundling he'd adopted, a baby someone had left under a hedge on his road to work, or the child of a secret lover my mother had before he married her. He never told me these stories when Mother was there, or when he was sober, and he rarely said the same thing twice – there would be slight changes, little details he would alter, from forgetfulness, or perhaps just to keep me interested. I didn't believe what he said, but I was upset by the intended cruelty, even when I'd told myself that it didn't matter, that I didn't want him as a father anyway. Ironically, there was no doubting our kinship. My mother would show me pictures of him, taken when he was a boy, and she didn't really need to point out the resemblance. If it hadn't been for the quality of the print, and the clothes he was wearing, I could have sworn the person in those photographs was me. He had the same lank hair, the same downward turn in his mouth, the same flat nose.

My father would talk for hours when he was drunk, telling me how he had to go out to work when his father died, how he never had the chances I was getting. He would tell me about my sister, who'd died in the womb, and I'd imagine her sealed eyes watching me in the dark. Sometimes his stories were interesting – like the time at the foundry, when a man called Tommy Hay got burned up, with everybody watching, and nobody could do anything about it.

'That was the worst thing I ever smelled,' my father would say. 'Nothing smells as bad as burning flesh.'

I didn't know if I believed him. The story had a second-hand feel to it, like most of what he said. It was as if he'd gathered together everything he'd ever heard in his life, in all the pubs he'd ever been in, and made a personal history of it all. When he was drunk, he would tell me about my real father, describing in detail how he died, on a wet Thursday afternoon in Edinburgh, or Fife. Occasionally this real father would fall from the Scott Monument while drunk; sometimes he collapsed in Princes Street Gardens and died in the hospital without ever regaining consciousness. Most memorably, he tripped and fell down the steps in Fleshmarket Court: he banged his head, then stood up, saying he was right as rain, but he was found on the train to Kirkcaldy, dead, or in a coma from which he never emerged. Nobody had as many deaths as my real father. He had five or six different lives to match, though they were less eventful, just years of working and drinking in Kirkcaldy, or Ladybank, or North Queensferry, where he occasionally drowned in the steel-grey waters of the Forth. His name was George Campbell; though my father never described him in any detail, I could see him in my mind's eye: a thin, wiry man, with narrow, horsy features – a face like a hatchet, my father would have said, being round-faced and a little fat himself. This man was dark where my father and I were fair; easy-going where we were irritable and nervy; skilful and quick to learn where we were clumsy and slow. I like to think this was my father's idea of him too; that we agreed, in silence, on this phantom's appearance and so made him real. Back then, I thought adults were autonomous: if my father behaved cruelly it was because he chose to do so;

I never imagined he told those stories because he was confused or unhappy. When he was sober, he sometimes brought me little presents, things I didn't want – a football, a second-hand fishing rod, even a puppy from his friend Mac. I accepted these things quietly, afraid of offending him, torn between pity and suspicion. I felt guilty for it, but those gifts worried me more than anything else, for I saw them as elaborate traps that I couldn't avoid. He'd give me something and I'd make a show of being pleased, but he'd see through the pretence, and it would only confirm what he'd suspected all along – that I was a stranger's child, fobbed off on him to make him look a fool. Even our physical similarity was a trick: the same hair, the same mouth, the same colour eyes. It was all too perfect, too close a match.

On Saturdays I would meet Tom at the corner of Union Street. If it rained, we'd sit in the bus shelter, watching the cars go by, but when it was fair we followed the old railway line into the woods beyond the derelict houses. If we had money we'd take the train along the coast and walk from pool to pool, looking for starfish. When we found an empty carriage, we'd sit in there, but usually we stood in the guard's van, listening to the pigeons. Often there would be four or five wicker crates full of birds: the men who kept homing pigeons along the line would travel up the coast and release them at various points on the way. The miners liked birds; those who didn't have pigeons built aviaries in their gardens, for the redpolls they caught in the woods. The trick was to balance a box on its edge then prop it up with a twig. You scattered crumbs under the box; the twig was attached to a long piece of string, and you would crouch in the bushes, holding the string, waiting till the bird flew down. When it went for the crumbs you pulled and, if you were lucky, you caught it. I tried it myself a few times, and I trapped a couple of linnets, but I had to let them go, because I had nowhere to keep them.

On Sundays my parents would argue about church. My father would say he wanted to go to the Kirk, though he wasn't a believer as far as I knew. My mother usually ignored him, but once she gave in suddenly and we stood for an hour in the Protestant church, not knowing what to do. My father was more awkward and embarrassed than we were. The Kirk didn't look like much to me, it was just a white room with people standing in rows, praying to empty space. Nobody seemed to know who God was. They didn't have pictures so you could see Him, with his heart on the outside, like in St Bride's. He wasn't really a person there, he was a spirit, like the wind that moved on the waters, or the voice in the burning bush. The Catholic church was better: it had pictures and candles, and the smell of incense. There were flowers everywhere, huge bouquets on the altar and little glasses of daffodils and grape hyacinths around the statues and the Stations of the Cross. I don't think I ever really believed in God as such, but I liked the incense, and the statue of the Holy Virgin, standing with her foot on the serpent's head, crushing it. Most of the saints had brown eyes and olive-coloured skin – I reckoned they must be Italian, like the De Marco twins – but the Virgin was fair-haired and pale, with bright blue eyes and arms spread wide, as if in welcome. I prayed to her when I prayed at all, but mostly I watched the priest and copied what the other people did, standing and kneeling at the appointed moments, impressed by the ritual and the sound of myself speaking Latin.

At night I would get up and go downstairs. I'd open the fridge, then I'd steal one of my father's cigarettes and smoke it on the back step, in my pyjamas. I'd be listening all the time, but I was never caught. I'd put a newspaper or a cushion on the step, so I wouldn't get piles, and I'd think about the stuff that bothered me, like what happened to people when they died, or why the angels couldn't have free will, or whether a ghost would feel solid if you touched it.

In summer I'd go out into the woods beyond the paper mill and hide among the rhododendrons. I'd pretend there had been a mysterious plague, and I was the only person left alive. When I went back there would be no one to stop me doing exactly what I wanted: I would move into a rich person's house and sit up all night, listening to foreign radio and smoking cigarettes; or I'd find a big car, a Jaguar, or a Bentley, and I'd drive up along the coast and sit on the cliffs, watching the sun go down behind the lighthouse.

The dare was to run barefoot through the field of nettles and hogweed between the farm road and the old slaughterhouse. You had to run as fast as you could: there was no stopping, no feeling your way to avoid the broken glass and rusty nails that might be hidden under the froth of blossom. When Will Dow ran it, he fell and cut his hand on a bottle, and Roly Rowlands had a long nail go through the sole of his foot, so he came out with a stigma, like Jesus. Everybody knew about that, but nobody refused the dare when their turn came. We all said the best thing to do was just to run, without thinking, splashing through the long weeds, with your eyes fixed on the slaughterhouse door. Afterwards you would rub your legs with dock leaves and say it didn't hurt, and if anybody asked you, you'd do it again, you swear to God, as long as they went too.

★　　★　　★

When it rained I took the bus to the pictures. I liked knowing people by name, the men in their good clothes, on their way to the club, the young women sitting together in twos and threes. I'd sit behind the Connolly sisters, or Sarah Pyecroft and her friend, so I could smell their perfume, and that gum Barbara Connolly liked to chew. The bus was warm and lit: people would get on and travel three stops, then get off and walk away in the half-light, disappearing into a distance as soft and grey as the afterlife we were promised in Scripture class.

The cinema was old and large, with red upholstery and dust motes floating in the petrol-coloured light from the projector. Most of the films were black and white, but sometimes the feature was in crude, bled-out colour. You could see anything – horror films, murders, love stories. I would sit in the hard, dusty seats, warmed and illumined by the story. When we stepped out later into the traffic and street light, the town looked vivid and bright in the rain, and we looked to one another like the people you meet in dreams, accidentally spilled into the everyday air. I liked the murder films best. I always wanted the murderer to get away and have a happy life far from the scene of his crime, but I knew he never would, and it was this that made him so beautiful, in the silvery light of the cinema. After a while, I realised that it was always like that; it was even a rule of some kind. The doomed characters were always noble and tragic; the righteous seemed narrow-minded and spiteful. When someone was killed it would rain, and the murderer would appear like a sleepwalker, crossing the lawn, or climbing in through an open window, always wet, always bathed in cold, dark water. I knew he wasn't really guilty; he was compelled to act by something beyond his control. The best murders were those where the victim died in his own house, standing in the bluish light of the kitchen: everything happens slowly, but without real violence;

the murder is part of ordinary life at home: pools of blood and water on the floor; a cold vapour breathed in your face, like when you opened the fridge; the sound of the wind; the shadow of leaves at the window. A moment later the body is laid out on the floor, or hunched in a chair with its last thought seeping away.

On the way home from school I would stop at Brewster's and pick up the paper. Nothing ever happened in that town, but my mother liked to read the announcements and cut out the recipes and knitting patterns. She would sit in the kitchen, identifying the people in the notices of deaths – teachers from her schooldays, people we knew by sight – and I would think of myself dying some day. Printed in the paper, death was real to me: factual, like the place names and dates in my school books. I felt sorry for my future self, and hoped I'd have a life worth remembering, for the sake of my wife and children, and everybody else I still hadn't met.

My father's death was unremarkable, one of those banal accidents that happen: a faulty pin, loose scaffolding, a fall of thirty feet from which he might just as easily have walked away. For a time there was talk of compensation, but it turned out that my father was as much to blame as anybody. The men had been told not to work in that section, but he hadn't been listening, and he'd gone over there for something – nobody really knew what had happened. The company offered a small settlement and admitted no liability. It was the kind of death my father would have imagined for George Campbell – sudden, pointless, unexplained. I tried grieving for him, but I couldn't separate him now, in death, from the real father he had invented. As I stood by his grave, as we drove away from the cemetery, as I sat in the front room and

listened to the funeral guests, I still wasn't sure who it was we'd buried.

When people talk about the past I feel uneasy. The past should be fixed, part of what I know about myself, but it shifts like mercury when I try to catch it, and it won't be still. Identity is only possible for the mortal; that is our gift. What I know about myself is uncertain and provisional: a childhood of tin and rain; an imaginary father; my teachers' voices revealing the shapes of the world by a process of repetition. I remember the uncles who drove me home in the dark; I remember sitting in the back seats of cars, watching the houses go by, the mystery rooms, the glimpses of lamplight and flesh. I remember the places close to home, where nothing happened for years, then sudden, unbelievable crimes were committed. I carry the thought of my addled sister, hanging in the womb, her eyelids and fingers waiting to be completed, and I remember my father saying he wished she had lived, and I had died in her place. I even believed I had stolen her life, that she really had died to make room for me. I would stand in the shops on George Street, while my mother chatted to someone she'd met, and I would look for the hairline cracks in my existence – random spills of flour and marmalade, the glitter of jars on the shelves, the betrayed look in the eyes of the fish when Mr Harris laid them out on the counter and gutted them with a neat, quick movement. One thing I know about myself: I am angry that my real father didn't exist and had to be invented, and that anger is heady and dangerous, something my body harbours, and turns against itself from time to time, like a private virus.

Mother is buried now, under the stone she chose for her husband, and I've inherited her custom of reading the births and deaths in the local paper and wondering about the people who have died. Sometimes, as I read, it occurs to me that most

of what I know about myself I have inferred from the presence of others. Even as a child my life was predicated on the many lives of my true father. I knew he was an invention and yet, without him, I wouldn't have been real. The dead are strangers now, but sometimes I can see them in my mind's eye, just as I see my real father, standing on the quay at North Queensferry, lighting a cigarette and looking out over the grey water. In the moment before his death I imagine him thinking of me, his long-lost son, and I think about how puzzled he must be, that we are so different. Once I thought of placing an announcement in the newspaper: *George Campbell, thirty-seven, suddenly, on 12th March, beloved father of Patrick, husband of Marie. Not dead, but sleeping.* I thought about it for some time, but in the end I let it go. I've no real proof he is dead and I prefer to think of him as missing, someone who might turn up one day, curious and friendly, a little remote, yet utterly unmistakable.

THE INVISIBLE HUSBAND

When I came home, that first night, the radio was playing at full volume in the kitchen. I heard it as soon as I opened the door: a deep, authoritative man's voice announcing the sporting results to a house I instinctively knew was empty, and I went through quickly to turn it off. There was no sign of Laura. It was already dark outside; I could see the orange and pale-green lights of the harbour, and the intermittent white of the lighthouse, flashing, then disappearing, across the firth. I went to the foot of the stairs and shrugged off my coat.

'Laura?'

I called loudly enough for her to hear me, even upstairs, at the top of the house, but there was no answer.

'Laura?'

The sound of my own voice worried me. It was too loud, too insistent. I suppose I already knew something was wrong; looking back, I see now that there had been signals I should have noticed, odd remarks and fleeting gestures that should have alerted me long before things came to a head, but I had tried to keep going, to pretend I hadn't understood, in the hope that the momentum of normal life would carry us through. I had been relying on that momentum for a long time; that was why I was so ill-prepared for Laura's illness. The secret of carrying on, the secret of that momentum, is to pay attention only to what suits you, and ignore every-thing else.

When I went back to the kitchen, I noticed the open door. I could have sworn it had been closed, only a moment before; now it stood wide open to the gathering night, and I stepped outside, into the cool clear air. Laura was standing in the middle of the lawn, in her white blouse and blue jeans, her head tilted, her eyes fixed on the sky.

'Laura?'

She moved only slightly, almost imperceptibly, but I was certain she had heard.

'What is it?' I asked.

She turned then, and I could see that she was smiling.

'Listen,' she said.

I stood quietly for a moment, listening, expecting to hear something out of the ordinary – a night bird, or music, or some atmospheric hum, but there was nothing.

'I don't hear anything,' I said.

She glanced at me, as if she had just noticed me for the first time, and was wondering who I was. That look scared me: it was as if she was deciding whether I was real or not, whether I was some illusion she had entertained for a moment, and was now dismissing. It was then that I noticed she was barefoot.

'You'll get cold,' I said. 'Come into the house.'

She turned away. Her shoulders and back looked thin; she had been dieting over the last several weeks and, for a moment, I thought she had overdone it, and made herself ill. It was one of the signs I should have noticed earlier, that obsession with her weight – she had never been fat, or even plump, but for some time she had complained about her body, standing in front of the mirror and worrying that her dress didn't fit, that she couldn't get into her jeans. For a moment, given this wisp of an explanation, the momentum of life resumed, and I was about to take hold of her, to bring her in and call the doctor, when she laughed softly and shifted away, lithe and quick as an animal, vanishing into the shadows by the hedge. I heard her laugh again, but I couldn't see her now, and it was a while before I realised that she had slipped through the gap in the wall and out into the cold, still night.

She came back about two hours later. The cuffs of her blouse were streaked with mud, and there was a long dark stain on her thigh; her feet were dirty and scratched at the ankles and heels, where she must have walked through brambles or thorns. Yet she had the same half-smile on her face as before, and when I asked her where she had been, she just laughed and stared at me, as if she still didn't quite believe I was real. I was at a loss. When I'd left her the previous morning, she had seemed fine; now she was acting like a mad woman. I ran her a bath and told her to get out of her dirty things and clean up, and she laughed again, but she did as she was told. In the meantime, I went downstairs to make myself a drink, thinking she would be a while, but after about ten minutes I heard her moving about upstairs and, by the time I reached her, she had gone to bed, still wet from the bath. I sat and watched over her for a while then: she seemed to be sleeping soundly, with her hands folded outside the covers, reminding me of a child, newly put to bed after a long hard day, and I didn't think it was a good idea to wake her. I was disturbed by her behaviour, of course, but I suppose, even then, that I blamed the whole incident on stress and told myself it would soon be forgotten, after we'd both had a good night's sleep.

I woke early next day. It was still almost dark, wet and windy, like a morning from childhood, when you wake too soon after a night of bad dreams and lie in bed, listening to the weather. I could hear Laura breathing softly beside me; I assumed she was still asleep, so I got up quietly and went downstairs. I had breakfast, then I called the office to tell Alicia I was sick. It was the first day's work I had missed for as long as I could remember and I couldn't think of an excuse at first – it felt odd to be lying, saying I had a cold coming on, and I was ashamed when Alicia was more sympathetic than I had expected, telling me to take it easy and not to come back till I was fully recovered. She would get Tom to keep an eye on the system build, she said, and Nicole could sort out the rest of the team. There was a moment – nothing much, just the slightest of pauses when she said Nicole's name – when I thought she knew what had been going on, and I was glad when she rang off. Just before she did, she told me again to take it easy and have lots of hot drinks, and I remembered that about her, that way she had of never getting through a conversation without offering a word of advice or encouragement. It was a trait that had annoyed me on occasion; now I found it endearing.

Nicole telephoned just before noon. I wasn't surprised, but it bothered me that she would take that risk and I suppose I sounded edgy when I answered. Laura was still asleep as far as I knew – I'd checked on her about twenty minutes before – but there was still the chance that she would wake and pick up the extension in the bedroom.

Nicole sounded uncertain of herself, but I couldn't tell if she was unsure of me, or just nervous because of the circumstances.

'Are you OK?' she asked.

'I'm fine,' I replied, and I noticed that my tone was just a little sharp. I paused a moment to listen for any movement overhead, before I continued. 'It's Laura,' I said. 'She's not well.'

'Oh.' She sounded put out, as if I had lied to her directly. 'I was worried.'

'Don't be. I'm fine, honestly.'

There was a longish silence. I felt paralysed, afraid I might say too much.

'Is it difficult to talk right now?' she finally asked.

'Yes.'

'Oh.' She still sounded upset, as if she thought I was putting her off for no good reason.

'We'll talk later,' I said.

'Fine.'

She hung up immediately, and I felt guilty, as if I'd dismissed her; nevertheless, I waited a moment longer, listening to hear if Laura had picked up.

The affair with Nicole was four months old, and already past its sell-by date. It had never been that serious – in fact, it had started almost as a game. She knew I was married, and at first it seemed nothing more than an elaborate flirtation, something we had been working towards for weeks after she joined the firm. I suppose I should have known the risks I was taking – perhaps I did. Looking back, I see how easily I managed to convince myself that our wager – that moment when things began to get complicated – was nothing more than innocent fun. It was simple: whoever got their system in first would be the other's guest at a local restaurant. As it happened, she won. That first night should have been enough to alert me to the dangers I was running, but maybe by then it was too late. Nicole was sharp, attractive, highly intelligent. We liked the same music, the same books. It was easy to enjoy her company, especially after a few drinks; later, as we were getting into the taxi home, she turned around and kissed me, her face tilted, her mouth dark and wet. All the way back to her flat, we ignored the driver and behaved abominably, kissing and petting like a pair of adolescents. When we stopped, she invited me in, and I accepted without a second thought. Upstairs, she went through the motions of making coffee for about three minutes, then we forgot all about that and went to bed. It was all very beautiful and strange and a little intense, like being sixteen again, vividly alive, and innocent of anything outside our own pure lust.

After that, we spent as much time as we could together. At home, I invented trips and late-night meetings so I could be with Nicole; in the office, we used every excuse we could think of to work on the same projects, so we could spend time away together. It was exciting, making plans, meeting in hotel rooms, sneaking back and forth in the night, but we were always discreet; Nicole didn't want anyone to know about us, not because I was married, but for her own reasons. For as long as the situation lasted, I don't think anyone really knew what was going on, even if Alicia had her suspicions. I felt guilty, of course; yet, in a way, it was Laura who had pushed me into the affair in the first place. I had always worked away from home, even before we were married; it was an essential part of the job. I was working in technical support then, so I had to be on client sites for days at a time, and if those sites were overseas, I might be absent for a fortnight or more, living in hotels and ringing home as often as I could. It was a hardship at first, but there was a pleasure, still, in calling her up and talking across time zones, having breakfast in Sunnyvale, in the clear Californian sunshine, and knowing she had just come in out of the wet and was standing in the kitchen, drinking tea, the raindrops still glistering on her face and hair. It felt right, somehow, to have to work at marriage – it allowed me a sense of gravity, of justness, when I came home after a job well done and we quietly resumed our normal life. In all that time, I don't think

I once suspected her of infidelity – the thought wouldn't have crossed my mind. I felt assured, and I expected her to feel the same way – not to take things for granted, not that exactly, but to feel safe and sound. Before Nicole, I had never been unfaithful to Laura – though I'd had my chances. As the years passed, the sex became less exciting, and I suppose my frequent absences put a strain on the marriage from time to time, but the rewards were still pretty substantial, and whenever we talked about it, in the early days at least, we agreed it was all worthwhile. My job paid for a nice house, in a nice neighbourhood, and a few luxuries besides. We had a pretty good lifestyle, all in all. If I was a little less intense than I had been when we were first married, that was all to the good: intensity had been replaced by a quiet, steady flicker, an assurance. I thought we were happy enough, under the circumstances.

I don't even know when the problems started. All I can say for sure is that, for more than a year before I even met Nicole, Laura was on edge, telling me I didn't love her any more, constantly complaining about my trips, more or less accusing me of an affair long before anything ever happened. When I had been abroad for a while, or if I came in late after a night out with people from the office, she would meet me in the hall, while I was still taking off my coat, and stand close beside me, sniffing delicately at my face and neck – my mouth, my hair, my shirt collar, even my hands sometimes, as if she thought I would come home with the scent of that imaginary woman on my fingertips. That upset me, to begin with, and I would try to think of something to say, something reassuring: I would tell her where I had gone, who else had been there, what we had talked about, even what I'd ordered. I would say I was sorry I was late, or offer to talk to Alicia so I could be away less often, but it was a waste of time. Eventually, I realised my mistake: the truth was that, no matter what I said, she already knew I was only saying it to cover my tracks, that I had probably rehearsed the whole story on the way home. Besides, I had only to mention one of the women in the office – Emma, or Christine, say – and she would know, just by the tone of my voice, or my furtive expression, that I was hiding something. Finally, I gave up: I would say nothing and just stand there, stock-still, while she checked me over for traces of a lover I didn't have. Ironically, it was about that time – about the time I gave up on her – that Nicole arrived. The attraction was instant: though I managed to hide it from myself for a while, Nicole told me later that she'd seen through my act right away – and maybe Laura had too. Maybe I had been giving out signals for a long time before anything happened: the affair was just the outward evidence, the explanation for a process of decay that we had been living with for years, without knowing it.

The strange thing was, we had started from a position of such strength. We had married just before my twenty-eighth birthday; Laura was just twenty-one. It had been a difficult time: my father had died the year before, and I suppose, looking back, I was trying to fill a gap, to resume something. I don't want to suggest that this was the only reason I fell in love – Laura was beautiful and intelligent, exciting to be with in those early days – but it was always there, half-suspected and only half-dismissed. Looking back, I can see that I wanted to be married – I had decided it, and everything I did was intended to reinforce that decision. Still, in those first few years, I delighted in everything about her: the way she dressed, the way she moved, her voice, the way she did her make-up or her hair. I woke in the night to watch her sleeping; I stole her perfume and dabbed it on my wrists so I could remember her when I was working away. Sometimes I drove all night and came home in the middle of the morning, after she had gone to work; I would come into the house and feel her recent presence there, her mixed scents, the dishes she had left, stacked neatly in the sink, the clothes she had discarded the night before. I would play the tape she had been listening to, taking up the music where she had left off. I would run a bath and lie there for hours, using her soap, her shampoo, her loofah. In the evening, when she came home and stood in the hall, hanging up her coat and scarf, I would ache with the desire to be her, just for a moment, just to know what it was like. I wanted to feel what she felt, see her dreams, think what she was thinking. In bed, I would lie beside her, my head touching hers, trying to listen in to her mind. When I asked her about it, she'd say she hadn't been thinking at all, and I would wonder what that was like, what it was to be absent, to be somewhere else. At times, I was jealous of that elsewhere – as jealous as I might have been of a rival. Yet even then, even as I succumbed to what I knew was folly, I also knew, somewhere at the back of my mind, that this was all theatre, a way to keep something alive, something I constantly suspected of being fragile and transient.

At the same time, I spent hours thinking about our future. I wanted to plan everything – not just pensions and insurance schemes and careers, but everything down to the last detail, to the holidays we would take when we had more time, to the places we might live when we retired, to how we would *be* together, the pleasures we would look forward to, the tests our marriage would survive. Once, when I had a minor eye complaint, waiting for my appointment at the Royal Victoria, I came across a man and a woman, walking in the courtyard garden that had just been planted next to the eye clinic. The nurse had told me I would have an hour or more to wait, so I'd gone for a stroll around the hospital corridors, stopping off at the Post Office and the book shop, lingering in places where the sick gathered, for the tastes and scents of their alien life, somehow so reassuring, so comforting. After a while, I began making my way back to the clinic and found myself in the garden. It was a warm, bright day. Even before I stepped outside I could smell the plants: carnations and lavender, lilies, roses, all the strong, sweetly scented flowers you find in gardens for the blind. There was no one else in the courtyard, just this man and woman, an old married couple who must have been together for years, so that every gesture, every word was minimal, just enough to convey what was needed. The woman, I assumed, was blind: she wore dark glasses and she was holding her husband's arm; whether from necessity or habit, she seemed to depend on him entirely – so much so, in fact, that he guided every step she took. Perhaps she had only just lost her sight, perhaps the loss of vision was temporary, yet it could as easily have been a game they had developed over months or years, another way of sealing their marriage, of binding themselves to one another. As they walked, the man described what he could see in an even, matter-of-fact tone: a yellow and scarlet rose-bud, a bed of petunias, a tall, evergreen shrub with spikes of red flowers and fine silvery foliage whose name he didn't know. The woman listened; from time to time, she would ask a question, then wait; the faint smile playing about her lips suggested that she was more of a gardener than her husband; that, while she enjoyed this walk in an imaginary garden, she was also humouring him a little. I watched them for a while, as they moved on, completely unaware of my presence, and I felt an odd pleasure, almost delight, at the idea of such a life. I could imagine myself with Laura, at their age, walking in a garden and sharing it, as they did. I could imagine myself, blind, listening to her voice, and seeing the flowers and the foliage, and the watery sunlight playing on the flagstones.

Finally, as they reached the far corner of the courtyard, the man looked up and, seeing me, gave a soft, apologetic smile, as if he felt he was depriving me of the garden in some way. At the same time, I couldn't help noticing the sadness in his face, a sadness he wanted to conceal from his wife at any cost. At first, I thought this sadness was nothing more than the predictable sorrow of a man whose wife's sight has been taken, perhaps unexpectedly, and I felt a surge of almost pleasurable compassion – for her, for them both, but most of all, for him, because he was the one who had to keep his real feelings a secret – he was the one who had to pretend. That pretence seemed beautiful, an act of love and nobility. Only after I had turned aside and began making my way back towards reception did it occur to me that the man might have been sad for another reason – sad, of course, for his wife, because she was blind, and because she was also pretending, but sadder still, sad to his very soul, for himself, because he was bound to her, by pity and habit as much as by love. I thought of my mother then, on the day Dad died: how she came home and tidied the house, and finished ironing his clothes, not for something to occupy her, as a distraction, but something done for its own sake – and I remembered the realisation I'd had at the time, that she wasn't really thinking of him, that she had already started the work of forgetting and moving on. The thought scared me, all of a sudden: I saw Laura, alone after my death, working to create an order I would never share, because it would give her a sense of herself as solitary and self-governing, not as a wife, but as a woman. When I went through to the examination room and sat, with my head in the frame, while the doctor applied drops and shone thin beams of blue light into my eyes, I thought of Laura, and I understood, for the first time, that I knew almost nothing about her, that, when I looked at her, what I saw was as much my own invention as anything else, a woman I had decided to love, for no good reason – as an act of faith, almost – a woman who could have been anyone, who could change at any moment, and might stop loving me on a whim, just as I might stop loving her, if chance intervened, or I no longer made the effort to continue.

Later that afternoon, Laura woke. I heard her moving about upstairs; when I went to see what was going on, I found her in the bathroom, still naked from the night before. She had brought down the potted plants from the top of the house and emptied them, soil and all, into the bath; when I found her, she was dragging a large fig tree across the landing.

'What are you doing?'

She looked up. She seemed surprised to see me, even a little frightened. She paused for a moment, then continued working, grabbing the fig by the trunk and pulling it towards her, eyes closed, as if she thought that I would disappear if she didn't look at me.

'Laura!'

I grabbed hold of the plant pot. As soon as she felt resistance, she let go and turned away; she was standing at the top of the stairs now and I suppose, in her bare feet, she slipped on the carpet. That was how she fell – I didn't touch her; I didn't even exert any force when I pulled away the plant pot. The fall was entirely accidental.

She wasn't hurt. She lay still for a moment, like an animal playing dead, then she scrambled back up and made for the front door. I caught her in the hallway: even though she was naked, I was certain she would have gone out if I hadn't held her back. I tried to hold on to her, then, to keep her from doing anything really crazy, but like Tam Lin in the old ballad, she seemed to change form, becoming an animal almost, as she struggled to

54

escape. Eventually, we ended up on the floor. I was sitting astride her, pinning her down by her arms, desperate, almost exhausted, and for an hour or more, I didn't dare let go. The phone rang twice; Laura seemed not to hear, or if she did, she pretended she couldn't. I tried talking to her, keeping my voice as calm and reassuring as I could manage, but she paid no attention – she wouldn't even look at me, twisting and turning every which way so I couldn't see her face. It was absurd. I could hear people passing in the street outside; I could hear cars and voices, children walking home from school, the dog at the pub, barking at every noise.

Eventually, the tension in her body dissolved and she lay still, as if sleeping. I relaxed my grip a little and she made no effort to escape. After a while, I struggled to my feet and stood over her, on guard, watching. She was more than still – she was inert, almost lifeless and, for the first time, in that moment's calm, I fully understood what had happened. All of a sudden, I felt cold and decisive: I fetched a throw from the sitting room and spread it over her, then I went to the front door, locked it, and put the key in my pocket, so she couldn't get away while I was phoning the doctor. Four hours later, we were on our way to the Royal Victoria and, that same night, she was admitted to Brookfields.

I have only the most fragmented memories of her time there. Every day – at work, or going around the supermarket, or driving home – I thought about her, imprisoned on the ward while the outside world continued, while the sun shone and the roses flowered and died in the garden, while the postman came and went, with letters for her, which I left unopened on the mantelpiece. I thought about her all the time – yet when I drove out there, I felt as if I was visiting a stranger. Most days,

I barely recognised her, though she hadn't changed that much. It was as if I lacked a sense of her, a focus that had been there before; I felt if I could just make some tiny, almost negligible adjustment, she would become real again, and I would see her as she had been when she was still my wife. I even thought I could bring her back from whatever limbo she inhabited, sitting there in the chair by the bed, or in the day room, her head tilted to one side like a bird's, as if listening for something faraway. Most of the time, she didn't talk or move, but sat by the window, with an intent look on her face; once, when the nurse brought me in and said gently – 'Laura. Your husband is here' – she looked up with a start and fixed her eyes on us. There was a flicker of life in her face for a moment, a look of excitement, of hope almost, then she turned quickly away, and resumed her vigil.

'That's not my husband,' she murmured after a pause, and it was clear that she was talking to the nurse, not to me. That was hurtful, of course: more so, perhaps, because I'd met Nicole that very day to tell her we were finished. She had been marvellous about it, but I knew she was disappointed. We'd sat in the theatre café for over an hour, while I tried to think of something more to say, some explanation for what had happened. If things had been different, I said – but she interrupted me there, and we'd finished the meal in silence, while the waiters came and went, asking if everything was all right, or if there was anything more they could bring us.

One afternoon, I took Laura out for a walk in the grounds. She had seemed fine when I arrived – she hadn't acknowledged me as such, but she hadn't rejected me either – and I had the idea that a walk would be good for her. To be honest, I felt more at ease myself in the open air; I always found the wards oppressive. It was a warm day; we crossed the lawn and stood by the cedar tree, in silence, like an old married couple, beyond the need for words. I felt almost content for a while; I was managing to convince myself that this was the first stage of her full recovery, when she began talking. It didn't make a lot of sense, but I gathered from what she said that there was someone – a man – who was lost somewhere, possibly in some kind of spacecraft; she called him by my name, but when I asked her if it was me, she laughed and shook her head, then went on talking. The man was lost, but he had made contact with her; now, wherever she was and whatever she was doing, even when she was asleep, that man was talking to her, and she was listening. If she stopped, he would be lost for ever: he would drift away into infinite space, and never return. The one thing that kept him in place, his one salvation, was the fact of her attention. I think she was proud of that. She felt the burden of her responsibility – and there was no doubt in my mind that she believed what she was saying – but she was proud, too, proud and fiercely glad, utterly convinced of the importance of her task. It was obvious that she had decided to let me in on her secret so that I would stop worrying about her, because she pitied me, even while she failed to understand why I was there.

For my part, I couldn't see why *she* was there. Within the usual limits, I think I understood the other patients. There were some young people, but most were middle-aged; they sat in the day rooms, or walked up and down the corridors in stale, shapeless clothes, waiting for whatever it was they expected to happen: a visit, or a death; release, or some deeper madness. At times, I think, they suspected themselves of acting. Even as they sat in their institution chairs, watching daytime television and sipping at weak, milky tea, they wondered if they were suffering nothing more awful than the daily disappointment, or the vague loss of equilibrium that troubled others from time to time, and that suspicion would provoke them to action – some piece of theatre, some diversion that would serve to convince both themselves and their imagined audiences that they were enduring a form of living hell. What troubled them most, I think, was the idea that anything is bearable, yet the only reason it was bearable was that, for them, time had stopped. I remember on one visit, I glanced out of a window and saw a woman in a night-dress crossing the lawn, heading for the cedar tree, with another woman in pursuit, not calling out, or even in much of a hurry, confident she would catch up before any harm was done. It was odd, how people did that: being pursued in some open place, they always made for a tree, or a building, like animals going for cover, as if they thought they would somehow disappear into the mass of this solid object, or at least be less visible, out of the light and the air. Because time had stopped, I knew there was something pointless about that woman's flight, just as she knew, even as she continued to run. It was as if it were nothing more than a rehearsal, with no real purpose, no possible end. Watching her, as she stumbled towards the shadow of the tree, her night-dress flapping in the breeze, I knew this scene would be replayed again and again, in the days and weeks to come. Nothing would ever change: not the stillness of the day room, not the pale green of its walls, or the man at the recreation table, mumbling softly to himself as he assembled, for the thousandth time, the puzzle he had been given by his daughter, a month, or perhaps a year ago.

But Laura was different. She should have been more resilient than those others; she should never have become the kind of person to allow herself the luxury of such descent; she should have known, as I did, that time continued because we willed it to continue. What shook me most was the idea that the woman I had married could even exist in such a place. I had always imagined people like us as strategists: while it was possible that we might be damaged by something unavoidable, something from outside, it had never occurred to me that the destruction could happen in our own house, while we ate and slept and went about our business. Every time I visited the hospital, I was shocked to realise that she had done this to herself, that she had let it happen and was letting it go on – that she had made it through the days, for weeks or even months, while I suspected nothing, giving no sign, but letting herself fall, slowly, to this point.

Nevertheless, she wasn't like the other patients. Even in the day room, she looked different from them: they were solid and dull, they appeared immutable, while she shimmered with light, no matter how lost or distant she seemed. That, I think, was what troubled me most: it was as if another woman, one I had never seen, was hidden in some fold of her mind, waiting to emerge, for reasons that had nothing to do with me. Sometimes I even believed – for seconds at a time – that the other man, her other husband, was real. While she was in the hospital, I began to wonder if I'd ever really known her, if, somehow, he had been there all along. It made me think we must always have been strangers at some level, when I couldn't decide what to say or do to help, or even how to be with her. No one had told me what I could or could not say. I'd expected some kind of guidance, but the nurses were noncommittal, and in all the time Laura was at Brookfields, I only saw one doctor, for about ten minutes. That was the day after she was admitted, when I was still confused; the proper questions didn't arise till almost a week later. Did I pretend everything was all right, or did I acknowledge her condition? When she told me I wasn't her real husband, was I supposed to insist that I was? When she looked on me as a stranger, was I supposed to scream and shout, and refuse to be erased from her mind – or was I supposed to go along with the idea that I was a phantom, that the real man, the real husband, would show himself sooner or later, finally realised, and ready to take my place? Then, when they decided she was on the road to recovery and would make quicker progress at home, was I the only one who suspected her of a pretence? Did the doctors really think that, in a matter of days, she had discarded her imaginary husband? Perhaps they did – after all, they had never known her, they had never met my real wife. How could they see, as they released her into my care, that I was bringing home a stranger? How could they know that the woman I had married had disappeared?

For several months, before I finally left, I lived with the woman who had been delivered into my charge. She went about her business, she functioned normally, but she lived in another house, with another husband. People – our friends, my former colleagues, even some members of my own family – despise me because they think I abandoned my wife at a difficult time, when she most needed me, but the truth is, I left because she had already abandoned me. The man she lives with now is her surest possession: he exists, somewhere, because she has saved him, he is tethered to her mind, to keep him from drifting away altogether, into the chill of infinite darkness. I have no idea who this man might be – perhaps he is the memory of a real person, some former lover or friend, perhaps he is a figment of her imagination, or even some twisted version of myself, a creature she has invented to fill the gap I must have left in our marriage. I don't know and, in those last several days, just before I left, I didn't really care. All I knew was, I had to get away, because that man, that invisible husband of hers, was beginning to become a reality, for me almost as much as for her.

★   ★   ★

60

On the last day, the day before I drove away, I was in the garden. It was Sunday: I had gone out, I suppose, with the intention of working, but by the end of the afternoon, I found I hadn't done very much at all. I'd pottered around with a trowel for a while, but mostly I'd just enjoyed being out of doors, listening to the birds in the neighbouring gardens, the gulls drifting overhead, the occasional harbour sounds. It was warm, but autumnal; I could smell winter coming, that faint, watery taste on the air, that suggestion of ice and smuts on the windows. Maybe it was the atmosphere, maybe it was just my frame of mind, but there was a fleeting and elusive moment when I felt someone was there – or rather, when I felt someone had been there, a split second before I turned, watching me from the other side of the garden. I don't want to make too much of it – I didn't actually see him, and I'm certain I imagined the whole thing – yet it shook me, and I felt a sudden wave of fear; or not fear so much as doubt: a dizzying sense of myself as imagined, as transient and insubstantial as any ghost, and I went indoors quickly, like someone fleeing a sudden rainstorm. The house was quiet and eerily still. Laura was asleep in the armchair by the fire; I saw that the book she had been reading had slipped from her lap, so I picked it up and put it face-down on the arm of the sofa. Before the hospital, she'd read novels and the odd book of popular psychology; now, she was into physics, theories of time and space, semi-technical volumes on the new science, full of references to Schrödinger's Cat and black holes. It was as if she was moving outwards, away from herself, towards some universal uncertainty which, by its very universality, became a law in itself. Such law was, naturally, indecipherable, but it was still law and, because it was indecipherable, it could never be refuted.

That was the day I decided to leave. I had already started

learning how to be alone, so the fact that Laura was never there, that she was already living with her other husband, no longer mattered to me. In one sense, I was the invisible one: as soon as I understood that home consisted of the inexplicable and difficult as much as the comfortable and familiar, and that nothing I could do, no effort, no mind-game or self-deception could alter that fact, I began to disappear. That was the day I decided to leave, once and for all, but in truth, I had already been gone for some time. As I stood beside Laura, unsure, now, if she really was sleeping, I reached out my hand and brushed my fingers across the wall, an idle movement, almost involuntary. The wall was covered with that old-fashioned, dusty paper that flaked to the touch, coating my fingers with tiny scales, like the flakes of silvering you find on oranges or moths' wings and, for a moment, the impression formed in my mind that the house was a figment of my imagination, something insubstantial, no more real than that husband of Laura's, or the fairy palaces in my childhood story books. It was an illusion that had been held in place by our marriage, by the aims and wishes and hopes we had shared there. Now that this illusion had collapsed, I could see that everything was just as illusory – the street outside, the parked cars, the shrubs in the garden – the idea of a world that existed because of some involuntary collaborative effort, a vague sense of shared reality that we had managed to maintain with one another, with the people at work and the postman and the couple next door. That impression only lasted a moment but, for some reason, it was as much a factor as anything in my decision to go. I almost laughed out loud when I realised what I had seen: it was a liberation, somehow, to think that I was part of an illusion, that even my sense of it as illusion was illusory, and I realised that, when Laura woke and saw that her book had been moved, she would think it was the other man who had moved it. Perhaps she wouldn't even notice that I was gone.

There is no way to explain this, not to the people at work, or the postman, or the couple next door, not to Nicole or my former friends, not even to myself. I could say something else, I could tell a different story entirely. I could talk as if it were a private myth, something I had put together from newspaper articles and scraps of hearsay: a man wakes early and slips away before anyone else is up, leaving his job, his wife, the house he has lived in for years. He is an ordinary man, cautious, and not in the least unconventional. He pulls in at the first garage to check the oil and the tyres, the way he would on any long journey, then he drives on, with no sense of urgency, aware of the light on the water as he crosses the firth, stopping here and there in the borders to notice how the landscape softens the further south he goes, the villages honey-gold in the morning sunlight, the leaves turning red or butter-yellow in the deep woods. He stays off the motorway as much as he can: there is something about time, something about being slow and easy, written into this journey – an escape, not only from the place that had held him for so long, but also from the sheer mass of his life, the bearable pretences of marriage and work and home. He is searching for something, for a stillness in his own mind, a new way of being that doesn't involve maintenance. It's something he has been ready to believe in all his life. As a child, he would have prayed to die in a state of grace, holding the image of some ice-clean purity of soul in his mind as he waited at the altar rail to take communion, dizzy with the smell of lilies and incense. I could say that grace is something he has expected, the one thing he trusts in an otherwise suspect world, a still from an old black and white film he once saw on television, a snow scene with pitched roofs and pine trees implicit in the distance. Naturally,

63

I have always imagined this man as a character in a story; he couldn't properly exist. It was a myth, this idea of departure, like the tale of the vanishing hitchhiker, or the crocodile in the sewer. Everybody wants to be someone else; we get so used to ourselves we hardly notice we exist. Some people want to be footballers, or opera singers, but all I wanted was to disappear. I never would have gone, if Laura's invisible husband hadn't come to take my place; in a way, I owe him a debt of gratitude. Even now, I think of him, moving quietly from room to room, setting things to rights, or standing in the garden, in the summer moonlight, speaking softly in my ex-wife's dreams. I have no way of knowing what he looks like, or if she even sees him, and I have never heard his voice, but I like to imagine, from time to time, that he looks and sounds like me or, if not me, exactly, then someone I might have become, once upon a time.

ETHER

On Sundays we would drive home in the dark, past the quarry and the black woods, our headlamps sweeping over fields of swede or kale, then beaming out into the darkness. Sometimes my mother would tell stories; sometimes she'd just talk about things, like how our lights would go on travelling into space, and never stop. I liked the idea of that but I never believed her. I would fall asleep for minutes at a time, then wake as we reached the first house lights on Grafton Road; from there, I would follow our route all the way home: past the graveyard threaded with mist or smoke in the orange light; past the empty playgrounds of my school, one for the girls and one for the boys; past the church; past Brewster's Newsagents and Tobacconists. I knew every door and gatepost on our street. I knew whose lights would be on, the light in the hall, or the light in the kitchen, and I loved those pale, goldish lights from upstairs, which always look warmer when you're on the outside. It made me feel good to think that every house had its own story, unwinding behind each window like a slow, mysterious film. I didn't want there to be any gaps. I remember when I first heard about the ether, how people had to believe in it once, because they didn't think light could travel through emptiness. For a long time after I knew they were wrong, I still believed they were right. It might not be true, but it was a better story, and that was what really mattered.

★   ★   ★

My childhood was a series of doubtful stories. I would hear them from my mother and her friends; I would hear them in church, or read them in the Sunday papers; when my mother gave me a radio to keep in my room, I would tune into tales of mayhem or terror, of haunted houses and ghastly murders that made my hair stand on end with delight. The thing was, all these accounts were supposed to be true. Or rather, unless the teller claimed some grounding in history, however slight, the stories meant nothing to me, and were soon forgotten. I remember one I heard, where a boy went out to fetch water from the stream in some remote northern settlement. When he didn't return his parents went looking for him, but all they found was the abandoned bucket, and a trail of crisp new prints in the snow that vanished into thin air, twenty feet from the water's edge. There was no sign of a struggle, no evidence to suggest someone else had been there and, on that still winter's day, when a dog's bark would carry from one parish to another, they'd heard no sound, no cry for help. For weeks afterwards, whenever I was sent out for coal, I would listen as I crossed the yard, expecting some winged creature to emerge from the white stare of the snow. I'd walk out to the pool in the woods and gaze into its depths where, leaf-black and still, the ancient drowned lay buried in mud, half-decayed, their skins partly tanned, their faces etched with the patterns of crowfoot and willow leaves.

Now all I want to do is to tell one story of my own. It won't be my story, as such; it will be more or less fictional, something that begins in the world, but ends up somewhere else, as an entirely mental event. Of course, if I could, I would write a whole book of stories, full of people like me, hoping for a different life, a state of grace, a cleaner way of being. I won't ever do it, though. I know my limitations. It may be that I choose them. Anyway, perhaps one story is enough.

Nevertheless, I would like to tell one story before it's too late. All I need is a space in the mind; a beginning, a middle and an end. Ideally, the story I tell will suggest a cleaner world – no less complex, no less subtle, just a world without the inevitable clouding of daily existence. I will tell my one story in winter, on the first day snow falls: I will sit by the window and say what I have to say, perhaps to a tape recorder, perhaps to an empty room. I may never write it down: the story might simply happen, as snow happens. I've always felt, watching snow, that what I'm watching is time. It's not like watching a clock: that's entirely artificial, an analogue; even if you remove the cover and gaze at the wheels and springs, all you see is a regular, contrived movement. Snow, on the other hand, is real time. The same flake never falls twice; no two are alike. The patterns are always changing. It's difficult to tell reality from illusion. In fanciful moments, I think of this as a representation of eternity, in the most perishable form possible. For personal reasons, I've been preoccupied with death all my life, which means I have also been preoccupied with eternity. You can't think about one without the other. I know there is something eternal in the world, but I wouldn't want to hazard a guess as to its nature.

That's why the story I will tell is only a variation on one that's already been told. I've considered others but, in the end, none of them works for me. For example, I've rejected the story of the exhumation of Thomas à Kempis. It defies belief that the man who wrote the *Imitation of Christ* was buried alive, then found, years later, his body twisted and wizened, the arms curled up under the coffin lid, each fingertip a robin's pincushion of splinters and old blood, where he'd scratched and clawed at the wood in his desperation. The irony is too obvious. Besides, I want my story to contain a resurrection of sorts: a small but significant triumph.

I am even tempted to repeat the story I heard from Silvia, one of my mother's friends, who had once lived in Italy – a story at once fanciful and everyday, concerning an old woman who had invited her to stay for a while at her country home. Silvia had been a sickly child, though by the time I knew her, she appeared in good health. The old woman, who had a great deal of money and no children of her own, had decided to more or less adopt Silvia and, for a whole summer, allowed her full run of the house and garden. The only place that was out of bounds was an old, dilapidated glasshouse, considered dangerous by Silvia's benefactor and, because it was forbidden, the ruin held a powerful fascination for a lonely child. She knew that every forbidden place has a story to tell – a dead lover, a ghostly woman, a murdered baby.

One afternoon, while the rest of the world was asleep, Silvia found a way into the ruined glasshouse and picked her way carefully through the litter of old clay pots and glass shards in the half-darkness within. The roof still hung with overgrown vines and wild trails of jasmine but, as her eyes became accustomed to the shadows, Silvia began to notice that, along one wall, in a neatly ordered row, several dogs lay, as if sleeping, with their muzzles turned up, to scent the air in their hunters' dreams, and their paws outstretched, the way her mother's dog slept at home, quite motionless, tensed and expectant. She always laughed at herself when she told how long it had taken her to see that the dogs were not sleeping at all, that their still bodies were dead and mummified, the eyes covered with coins, the skins dry as parchment. She ran from the place in horror then, cutting her hand on a piece of glass; the first person she met was the old lady, who took her back to the house and got her to calm down. The next day Silvia was sent to the priest, to make her confession, and nothing more was said. Silvia used to say she still had dreams about those dogs. That's why this story belongs to her still and, besides, it suggests nothing more than death's stillness, and the story I want to tell must contain a resurrection. It has to be something familiar, something I know – perhaps it's nothing more than an atmosphere: a crispness in the air, like the space over a football pitch in autumn, drifts of copper leaves, echoes, a strangeness in the wind when it touches my face, reaching out from some unimaginable distance. It has to be one of the first stories I ever heard, the one I had suspected all along. The story I want to tell is this: that, beyond the rain, beyond the fields, beyond the fuzz of snow on the kitchen window, Lazarus is still in the tomb, waiting for someone to call him out, waiting to wake again.

Several versions of the Lazarus story are possible. The first, and most obvious, is a waking body, dusted with ice, breathing and moving again, returned to the living and, at the same time, suspended, like a foetus in a jar, perfectly preserved, in an odourless, colourless medium. This was the version I wanted to believe, the story in the textbooks. I could picture Lazarus as he was, raised to a world of cuttlefish and bees, to foreign utensils and food he could no longer stomach. Or I could imagine him at night, when his sisters were sleeping – the midnight feasts of sugars and tainted meat, bowls filled with elvers, oysters sucked from their shells. It was difficult to shrug off this image of a resurrected body: the slow and painful unwinding of the bandages, the whitish mycelium of pus and sweat on the skin and the first hint of decay: a bruised look, the blood that had been still for days only just beginning to quicken. In this resurrection, the dead man's eyes have already clouded;

71

it will be weeks before the numbness seeps away through his fingers and, with it, the sweet comfort of inertia. It was an effort to replace this image with another, simpler idea: a deliberate heresy in which Lazarus is alone in a white interior lit with candles, rehearsing his own death and rising again – lying still for three days, listening, suspended in the heat. Like anything else, resurrection would require practice. Many died and did not return. Lazarus was caught in the space between death and rebirth and had to be drawn back home by Jesus. In one version of the story, he does not come back, but remains, beguiled by the silence, or by the music he thinks he can hear beyond the grave; and the one who returns in his place, though he resembles Lazarus outwardly in every respect is, in fact, his antithesis.

So it is that, at the end, when Lazarus is alone in his dying and even his sisters have receded into the surprising depths of the sick room, he dreams several times that he is standing in an empty place, like the room in the temple outside the Holy of Holies, which no one is permitted to enter. There is a veil in this room and behind the veil is a light – the only light he sees in the dream, shining through the thin, almost transparent fabric. This light is close, but it is not local: Lazarus knows it extends beyond the veil in every direction – his impression is of something boundless. What is local is a figure, a form like his own, sometimes beyond the veil, enlarged by distance, sometimes so close that the material clings to its face and hands when it presses forward as if to push through and enter the cool room where Lazarus stands, fascinated. This figure resembles him, but in the dream he knows it is not Lazarus: it is a life that would assume any form in order to exist.

When he wakes, there are women around the bed. They pour water into a stone bowl and one bathes his face while the others stand apart in silence. It occurs to Lazarus that there is no sound

72

in the sick room, or even outside, in the garden he knows so well, where birds and cicadas should be singing. The dream is also silent. He wonders if this is a condition of his death and whether he would survive if he could hear something. When the woman finishes and stands back he sees her lips moving, and he strains to listen. But there is no sound, and a few moments later he is in the other room again, watching the shadow move behind a lighted veil.

I am trying to remember an afternoon in summer, but the memory is too formal, and it keeps me at a distance. I see in detail the broken wall of the churchyard, the rows of pines and stones, the brilliant reds of fresh carnations and the faded pastels of silk flowers on the graves. It was a Sunday, very warm in the sun, so the shade seemed cooler and darker: I remember a faint scent on my skin and the half-fever of the heat. I have an impression of being far inland, away from the cities, in a place where nothing ever happened – as if that place were a kind of paradise, where people lived their allotted years and died of old age, half-smiling, like children exhausted by a long party, falling asleep and waking in the next parish, with new names and faces, knowing what life would bring and ready to repeat it again.

There are several possible resurrections, but the one I find easiest to imagine is the partial return of floating unseen over a garden still thick with memorised details: a return that could easily be an hallucination, where nothing is new – abandoned cups of tea and brackish water on the steps; a silent child, self-absorbed among the hostas and ferns; colonies of ground elder pressed to the garden wall, probing the bounds, finding cracks. I can imagine floating in the summer light, the sensation of being closer to the distance than to the house and garden below, the sensation of being pulled, as if caught in an undertow, away from the red peonies and mown grass, towards the empty pine trees in the hill, the dry slopes of sand and gorse, the cool darkness, silence.

When Lazarus wakes, inside the tomb, there is noise. It is not the broken sounds of the day he hears; this noise is a flow, as continuous as night. At first he thinks this river of sound is no longer happening – it is something that has remained printed on his mind like black footprints after someone has crossed wet grass – but after a while it begins to change and he knows the sounds are real: splashing cries, hushed voices, the sounds of mourning in its last stages. It is a sublittoral world beyond the stone: he finds things there he has never heard before. When the people move away they are replaced by birdsong, and he turns back to himself, to the bird-smell of his dead body, the tightness of his skin, a thread of sweetness in his throat as if he had recently swallowed honey. From time to time he sleeps, or seems to sleep. When he wakes, or seems to wake, he is waiting for something. Sometimes he has the unexpected feeling that a child is the tomb beside him, asking questions he cannot answer: does memory reside in perfumes or sounds? are some pieces of time identical? does everything flow away or does it stand forever, perfectly still?

I understand that the dead are naked. They remember nothing: as soon as the graves are sealed, they begin moving away from their loves and griefs, forgetting their houses and gardens, forgetting those episodes on crowded streets, when their bodies were drenched with cold or the beating of wings, in a dizzying moment of foresight. They are walking away in a field of barley, chest-deep in warmth and undertow, feeling their bodies stray with each tug of the wind and thinking it no great loss, to

74

begin again. It's important to admit that these named individuals disappear. We know they go into darkness, it's the only way they could ever start over. They go into darkness and whatever it is that continues goes on without them. Something they borrowed, some scrap of soul or grace, something that was never theirs alone – whatever that is – survives. Even the faithful suspect this is true. They talk about the soul, they pretend it's a personal matter but, in their hearts, they know the soul is only immortal because it belongs to no one. It keeps taking the form of an individual, but the only way it can persist is to shed that form, the way a locust sheds its skin and emerges, glistening, into the new.

Lazarus has become aware of something that is too large for the limited space of the tomb. He waits to recognise this presence: he wants to see, even if it is hideous, or terrifying in its beauty. He wants to give it a name. This is the constant temptation: to use the name of a god, to make it life-size and personal, just as it is a constant temptation to see the soul as an individual belonging or property. Even though he knows these things belong to nobody, Lazarus wants to pin them down, and he is surprised when he realises the word he is searching for has slipped his mind. The harder he tries to remember, the stronger his sense of the presence becomes, until it fills the space inside the tomb, encompassing him, even while it has no form or dimension he can describe. It is perfectly dark and silent in the tomb, yet Lazarus is aware of the garden beyond the stone, the sounds of birds and running water, the perfumes and colours, the textures. He knows the presence is outside too. It is not a dogma; it is not something he chooses to believe.

Later, people come to roll away the stone. Lazarus rises and walks into the heat. When he reaches the entrance, his first act is to turn, to see what was there beside him in the dark. The tomb is empty. Or at least, nothing is visible. He expects as much and is grateful he could not remember the name of his god. When he turns back to the crowd, Jesus is standing before him. He sees no one else, only Jesus, and for a moment he understands that Jesus is more Lazarus than Lazarus has ever been. At the same time, he knows it was Jesus beside him in the tomb, keeping him awake, till the man he knows as Jesus could travel from Betharaba, beyond the Jordan, to raise him from the dead.

I remember being at home, then I remember being somewhere else, but I have no memory of leaving. All I know is the stories suddenly stopped. I remember the houses and the churchyard, but no people except my mother and her friends – though strangers sometimes came, in wet or dusty cars full of children and dogs, in a strange and compacted space that seemed pressed against the rear and side windows, a space they carried with them all the time, smudged with rain and motorway lights. The people came to see the church, which was partly Saxon, but they always seemed to find less than they had expected. Perhaps they had read a description in a tourist guide and assumed it would be prepared for their visit, specially cleaned, cheerful with bells and a choir.

  In reality, the church was silent, and almost empty of decoration. Sometimes it was locked. When they did get in, the people found a cool, whitewashed space with an altar at one end and a plain glass window at the other. Some folded xeroxed sheets lay on a pine table by the door: a history of treasures owned and lost. The people looked, walked about, touched things, and went home disappointed. What they missed was everything the guide books omitted: bottles of greenish water in a stone coffin;

a besom in the corner; a handbrush and a dustpan full of dried leaves and beetle shells; the wet, mould-stained patch on the wall where the holy spirit burrowed through in the night.

Later, if it rained, the air would close around us and we were each alone in a separate part of the house. We could not stay together. We would drift into corners and alcoves, or stumble upon one another, like strangers in the house, reading in a window seat, or behind a curtain. I would sit on the upstairs landing, looking out at the trees in the churchyard. It was as if the rest of the world had disappeared, and I was glad. I could imagine we lived on an island, surrounded by something I could almost feel on my skin, a medium the light or the wind could enter and roam in at will, sliding in to touch me then moving away again, leaving only the faintest afterprint on my skin, as if something had gripped me gently then, just as suddenly, had let go.

After his resurrection, Lazarus stays in the garden. It has changed, he thinks: the sound of the stream that feeds the pool is subtler, or more variable; the shadows under the trees are deeper and cooler. He stays outside: even at night his sisters cannot persuade him into the house. It is not that he fears the closed space of his room: nothing reminds him of the grave, but he wants to feel space above him, the slight pressure, the special quality of being visible that he only experiences out of doors. By day, the temperature is almost unbearable, and the sisters feel that Lazarus is somehow implicated in the heat, for how else could he sit motionless in the full sun? By night, they watch him from the house, waiting for something to happen, the beginning of some ordinary event, some gradual return. It seems he never sleeps, but he is so still, so quiet, that he might be sleeping all the time. Sometimes they think he is aware of being watched: a white, formalised being, like some lesser Egyptian god, part–cat, part–moonlight.

What he remembers now is something he has never seen. There is no sound attached to his memory; the image is one that was passed on to him by a sea–trader he had met years before: an image so hard and precise he can hold it in his mind and turn it over, like a piece of driftwood, or a pebble. The trader had spoken of a people who bred children in glass jars, using a secret mixture of seaweed and blood. The children were born with bright green eyes and golden hair; they were treated as the favourites of the gods, living freely in the temples; then, at the age of twelve, they were sacrificed to the spirit of tides.

Lazarus does not believe this story, but he is struck by the idea that the soul is a glass, or a creature bred in glass, a beginning, a birth. What you expect to grow there, grows: a thread of blood, smears of tissue and keratin, muscle and tendons, brain, liver, heart. Tiny mouselike bones; webbed hands; veined, hairless skin stretched tight across the skull, the eyes clenched, black under the finely wrinkled lids; the mouth toothless, sucking air. You expect it to be an imago, finally, of yourself, and you are surprised when it has a life of its own behind the veil: its own waking; its own thoughts; its own hunger.

After the resurrection, Lazarus lives a life of grace, not because he has died and been raised, but because he knows there is no secret in the grave. The only secret is the one he has refused to admit all along: the noises in the dark he hears now every night: a light metallic tapping like finger cymbals, a series of thin, dry whistles, too erratic to be intended as music, the breathing of entire armies beyond the garden wall. Other noises: a confused babble at first, but there always emerges a single convincing sound: someone is walking steadily towards him out of the darkness, moving closer and closer, someone else at first, then

Lazarus himself, returning, finding his place, ready to begin the work of forgetting.

The sisters watch. They cannot believe his body is unmarked, that it is possessed of an almost impossible cleanness, and they watch for some sign of decay: fissures in the skin, a stickiness, the first bad odour. They keep expecting him to speak, to tell them the story of his death. But Lazarus is silent. Nothing reminds him of death, but he has a partial memory of the soul or rather, not the soul, but the idea of a soul, half-pulse, half-wound, like a skylark's song-threaded larynx.

DECENCY

The hashish seller was in his usual place under the arch, not far from where the carriage drivers gathered to call to passers-by, in quiet, yet insistent voices, offering tours of the town, or short drives along the coast road. The hashish man was just as quiet, but he had an effete, almost pleading manner that Robert had begun to find very irritating. For no good reason, he had disliked the little man from the first – though he'd been tempted, a couple of times, by the idea of a smoke on his solitary walks around town, while Sandra lazed in the hotel room, reading airport novels, or soaking in a hot bath. Now, only five days into the holiday, he almost hated this scrawny, pathetic little man, just as he almost hated the carriage drivers with their grey, tobacco-stained whiskers, and the rude woman who watched from the kiosk on the corner, observing him openly, without even trying to conceal her suspicion that he was up to no good. He didn't know why these people annoyed him so much: it wasn't their fault that they had to make a living, any way they could; it was just something about their presence at the edge of the plaza, something about the damp physicality of their bodies that repelled him, as much as the ratty dogs in the side streets did, or the bad-meat smell around the butchers' shops, and he couldn't wait to get to his hiding place among the rocks.

As always, it was too hot. Sandra wouldn't go very far in the middle of the day, so he had begun taking these walks by himself, around the plaza at first, just to be out in the light and the air, then later to the rocks, high above the beach, away from the people. After a short morning stroll, Sandra would stay in the room for the best part of the day, or she would sit reading in the narrow tree-lined square opposite the hotel, stilled and dark and self-forgetting. Robert envied her that, the way she could just switch off and be absorbed in a book, or a talking tape; at the same time, he couldn't understand why she had chosen this, of all places, for a holiday. Since she disliked the heat so much and resented the attentions of the carriage drivers and the little hashish man even more than Robert did, he wondered why she couldn't just stay at home, in the back garden, with real tea on hand and an endless supply of novels from the public library. She would have been happier there. On the one excursion the town had to offer – a morning's trip to the local caves – she had complained about everything: the damp, the artificial lighting, the absurd music. True, a great deal had been done to spoil the effect of the caves, and the commercialism was, to say the least, annoying: as soon as they entered the first dark cavern, two photographers had stepped forward to take their pictures, flashing bright lights in their eyes and blinding them, and later, when they emerged, and the hard-sell began, Sandra had been so angry that they had walked back quickly to the coach, without even stopping for coffee. Yet the caves had been beautiful, in their own way, and Robert had found himself appreciating the place, in spite of himself: nothing could quite spoil the effect of the huge stalactites, dripping with chill, primeval water, or the sense he had of the people who had once lived there, making fires and eating animals in the dark, infinitely alert, aware of every shift of movement and scent in the air around them.

The next morning, Sandra had found a second-hand

bookshop, around the corner from the hotel, and she had withdrawn into her own small world, just as she always did, leaving Robert to his own devices. Which wasn't saying much: the town was one of those semi-unspoiled places that look good compared to Malaga or Torremolinos, but the beaches were gritty and narrow, and crowded, where crowding was possible, with German and British holidaymakers, middle-aged mostly, away from home and revelling in the free vulgarity it allowed. To begin with, the place had appalled him, and he'd wanted to give up and go home; then, by chance, he had found the rocks.

His sanctuary was really little more than a ledge, perhaps forty or fifty feet above the sea. In some ways, it was an inhospitable place – but it was a place where no one else would choose to go, and that made it exactly what Robert wanted. Up there he could lose himself in the noise the waves made crashing against the cliff face below, and he listened intently to the sound, as if hearing it for the first time. The rocks were ugly – they resembled huge chunks of concrete, or pebble-dashing – and they were far from comfortable, but they at least allowed him that sound, that grand noise of the sea, of something larger than the world of the town. The spot he had chosen was around twenty feet from the path, and where he sat, obscured by some scrubby trees and a large boulder, he could sometimes hear the voices of passers-by – the French, the Germans, the Spanish, the English – but he himself could not be seen. That might have been the best thing about the place: he hadn't come there so much to be alone as to be invisible. He wanted to think of himself as a neutral observer, like that ideal character in elementary science books who stood apart from the experiment he was conducting, and simply measured and recorded what he saw.

It was odd, this choice he had made. He didn't entirely

understand why he enjoyed the rocks so much, but all he needed was to spend an hour or so there each day, listening to the waves, and watching the lizards as they angled across the rough stones, dodging into the sunlight, then vanishing back into the shadows, always tentative, always cautious, scenting the air, their thin, brown and gold bodies finished with a long turquoise tail and glittering in the sunlight, as if they had been forged in a jeweller's shop. There was even a consolation to be had from the slight sense of personal danger, from the fact that, as he leaned out over the beating waves and listened, there was some corner of his mind that could appreciate the idea of a fall, if only for the satisfaction of seeing it happen – not because he wanted to be injured or killed, but because the pull of gravity was so pleasurable, so absorbing, and the longer he sat up there, on his sunlit eyrie, the stronger it became.

Later, walking back to the hotel, he became aware of a new sensation: an odd, near-palpable pressure on the surface of his skin, a tight warmth in his face and scalp that brought to the surface something old and residual, a sluggish, reptilian element deep in his flesh, slowly coming to life. He had noticed it before, though it had never been so acute: it was something detached from any human concern, something neutral, or even alien: the more it awoke, the more he felt himself altered, receiving signals and stimuli he normally missed – a gust of scent on the air, a flicker of movement among the hibiscus shrubs at the square's edge, a new resonance, or some bright splash of noise in a side street, that sent tremors through some fine cord in his spine that he had never been aware of until that moment. On the one hand, the sensation left him feeling more alive, more rooted in the world; on the other, he was aware of a vague frustration, as if some age-old power had curdled inside him,

lost and unexpressed, wasting away. He felt vaguely that Sandra
was somehow to blame for that, but he could not have said why.
He only felt certain – in a quite consciously melodramatic way
– that she was the secret enemy of this power, just as he felt she
was the secret enemy of all his desires, and even of his deepest
sense of self.

He didn't want to go back to the room. He knew Sandra
would be there, but that wasn't the only reason. It was one of
the things he disliked about holidays, the way everything was
reduced to the banal: the dog that barked all afternoon on the
opposite balcony, the absurd food they had to eat – unclassified
fish steeped in brine, wafer-thin cuts of meat smeared with
dried herbs and cream – even the idiotic love-songs they heard
wherever they went. It all served to remind him of contingency,
of the awkward reality of the flesh. If he went back now, Sandra
would be there, sitting in the bath with a romantic novel, or
wanting to go to the bar, where he would have to endure the
inane conversations, the slow, too-deliberate slurping of coffee,
the attentions, or the inattention, of some cherubic waiter. He
didn't want to go back and, although it was almost time for their
evening drink, he decided he wouldn't. Instead he walked to
the tourist offices, picked up the local English-language paper,
and found himself a free bench on the Balcon de Europa, in
the thin shade of some palms. He could still feel that vague,
animal warmth on the surface of his skin, and he wanted to
make the moment last a while. Strangely enough, and in spite
of its position, the Balcon was one of the most peaceful places in
town. Perhaps the view, with its wide panorama of calm sea, or
the intensity of the light, or the endless murmur of cicadas made
people self-conscious, but children played quietly here, being
good for ice-creams and cold drinks, while the adults moved
slowly, languid in the heat, dreaming of some more sensual

state, some fantasy of the Mediterranean. Even the hashish man would not approach, so long as Robert remained seated.

The paper was little more than a rag, like the free papers back home, full of adverts for shops and services along the coast, but there were two or three cultural items, articles on the *Concurso de Flamenco*, and a short piece about the local arts scene. A woman from Cadiz, it seemed, had mounted an exhibition of childbirth-related photographs in Malaga, with nude scenes and honest, uncompromising images of the process, from first to last, and this had caused controversy among the ex-pats, retired accountants and underwriters who found the pictures offensive. There was a photograph of the artist, a frank-looking, slightly bemused woman, with deep, pretty eyes, and a quote from the provincial head of culture, who declared that art could have no limits. The article took up most of the middle pages; directly below, in a near-throwaway paragraph, a short news item appeared:

> *The body of a young woman was found on the beach out-side Almeria on Monday. The victim, apparently a prosti-tute, is the sixth to have met a violent end in the province in the last several months. The fifth was found beaten to death in her flat in the city just two weeks ago. The police remain baffled, although suspicion exists that a serial killer may be at large.*

The item looked strangely out of place at the foot of the page, among the bridge club announcements and advertisements for video rentals; for some reason, perhaps because it was told so simply, without the smallest hint of compassion, Robert found it strangely shocking. He read it again and, then, as if he felt he could purge the images it had raised in his mind by doing so, he read it through once more, very slowly. He couldn't help imagining the girl, thin, dark, with runny make-up and wet bruises around her eyes and mouth, and he felt a sickening rush of tenderness and longing – not for her, whom he did not know, as much as for something abstract, something unsayable. He looked up. At the far end of the square, by San Salvador church, a funeral procession had begun to assemble and, in a moment of confusion, he imagined it was for the murdered woman. The hearse looked absurdly out of place in the late afternoon sunlight, as people walked by in shorts and T-shirts, eating ice-lollies; beside the coffin, among the carnations and wreaths, Robert could make out a simple black and white sign, which read 'Funeral Nacional, Nerja'. At that same moment, a man approached. He was about forty, tall and supple-looking, with thick, reddish-brown hair. Robert noticed, in that first moment, the sheer intensity in his eyes, an immovable quality that, in another place, might have seemed threatening.

'Good afternoon.' The man's voice was soft, quiet and easy. For some reason, perhaps because the stranger had such a deep, finished-looking tan, Robert was surprised at his being English.

'Good afternoon,' he replied.

'I noticed you were reading the paper,' the man continued, 'and I wondered if you might do me a favour.'

Robert nodded almost imperceptibly. He did not wish to appear inhospitable; at the same time, he wanted to make it clear that he was enjoying his own company. It turned out, however, that the man's request was quite trivial. He said he had lost his own paper and wondered if he could borrow Robert's. Robert nodded again, and handed him the paper – at which point, the man sat down on the bench and began to study the middle pages. After a few moments, he turned to Robert and smiled.

'I was curious,' he said. 'I saw the item, and I wondered what it was about.'

'Ah.' Robert nodded. 'The exhibition. I suppose you have to expect that kind of reaction–'

The man laughed softly, and shook his head.

'No, no,' he said. 'It was the murder I wanted to know about. The girl.'

'Oh.' Robert glanced at the paper, which the man was now folding neatly into four. 'I see.'

At this point, the stranger introduced himself. His name was Gold, he said; he had been living in Spain for some time; the reason he had been so interested in the paper was that he was a keen student of police work – 'strictly as an amateur, of course,' he added, with a smile.

'The Spanish police are cleverer than you might think,' he continued. 'They know much more about this case than they pretend. Yet they say nothing.'

'I see.' Robert did his best to appear polite, without seeming to concur, either way, in Gold's estimation of the authorities.

Gold laughed again.

'No, no,' he said, 'it's quite true, believe me. I've been studying these cases myself, in a manner of speaking, and I can honestly say that the killer has left many more clues than the police have admitted. Unless, of course, they haven't found them.'

'I don't understand.' Robert felt himself tumbling into a trap, yet couldn't resist the provocation. 'How would you know about them, if they haven't been found?'

The man smiled.

'Because,' he said, in a matter-of-fact way, 'I put them there.'

He stood up and hovered a moment, the folded-up paper

poised between his thumb and forefinger. The intensity hadn't dimmed in his eyes, yet Robert was surprised at the way the man managed, simultaneously, to be smiling – a thin half-smile, polite, reassuring, designed to put him at his ease, in spite of what he had just said.

'Mind if I keep this?' Gold asked.

Robert shook his head; then, confused, murmured his assent. He experienced a surge of giddiness, coupled with a profound desire to escape, to be alone and at home, watching television in his own sitting room.

'Thanks.'

Gold smiled warmly, as if Robert had just told him the latest football score, and turned around.

'See you again,' he sang out, as he walked away, across the sunlit square.

The next evening, when Sandra took to her bed with a copy of *Gone with the Wind*, Robert decided to go to the *Concurso de Flamenco* at the Colegio Municipal. He didn't really know anything about flamenco, but he had no intention of hanging around in the room, trying to block out the noise of the dogs and the mopeds in the street below. He assumed flamenco would be some kind of guitar playing, with women dancing and clapping, or swirling around darkly in red dresses. The *concurso* didn't start till ten thirty, so he strolled along one of the sidestreets off the square and walked into a dim, tidy bar for a drink.

It was one of those bars that had once been for the locals and was now converted almost entirely for tourists. Large sides of ham were suspended among the roof beams; the walls were decorated with the usual bullfight posters and a portable CD player pumped out sevillanas. Robert sat down at a table and ordered a beer.

The bar was almost empty. An elderly couple sat in one corner, looking edgy and uncomfortable, not only with their surroundings but also with one another. The woman had a thin, pale mouth, and she was somehow meagre-looking, like the lizards Robert had seen on the rocks; the man was smoking, sipping at a beer, his hands busy, a desperate look in his eyes. At the end of the bar, the waiter, a local, was trying to flirt with a couple of pretty, slightly tipsy blonde girls. The conversation was a mixture of Spanish and English: one of the girls, the one closer to Robert, was drunker than the other; she was also the prettier, and Robert found himself watching her furtively, the way he often did when he was alone in bars or restaurants.

The girl looked around twenty, perhaps slightly older; she was wearing a thin, low-cut beach dress and sandals. She was very well tanned, for a blonde, and her bare legs were covered with a light silvery down. She had the kind of body that seems suspended halfway between girl and woman, almost boyish even, but her mouth was dark and sensual, and her voice was charged, musical without in any way being sing-song, deepening and spreading when she laughed to include everything and everyone. After a while, when she was certain that Robert was watching her, the laugh, and her conversation, gradually broadened to include him, and she began throwing him quick, sidelong glances. Robert found himself trying to smile – naturally, casually – whenever she looked his way. He was considering whether he might approach her – if he went over to the bar for another drink, he might reasonably go to where she was standing, since the barman was also there – when he felt a slight pressure on his arm. He looked up.

It was Gold. On seeing him, Robert felt a surge of panic, but the man only smiled, and sat down.

'Hello, again.'

Robert glanced back across the bar at the girl. She was looking away, talking to her friend. Gold laughed softly.

'It's one of those places,' he said quietly, with a note of insinuation in his voice.

Robert stood up. He wanted to escape, to walk away, then he remembered that he still hadn't paid his bill. He looked for the waiter, who was still hovering around the English girls, then he turned to the elderly couple, who turned away quickly. Quietly, without a fuss, Gold reached out and took hold of his arm.

'Sit down, Robert,' he said. If anything, his voice was softer than before, but now there was a darker note, a contained threat. Robert sank back into his seat.

Gold set his elbows on the table and regarded him with interest.

'How do you know my name?' Robert asked.

The other man ignored the question. He seemed to be thinking, trying to remember something.

'Did you ever have that sensation,' he said finally, sounding as if he were about to tell a story, relaxing, settling in for it, 'did you ever have that sensation, visiting a foreign city – on business, perhaps, or shopping, or killing time between trains? How you suddenly realise that the city is familiar, and then you remember it's the home of an old friend, someone you haven't seen for years, and towards whom you feel a vague, slightly resentful guilt?'

He paused a moment to give Robert a questioning look. Robert shook his head and turned away. The girl at the bar was perched on a stool now, with her back to him, in deep conversation with her friend. Gold continued talking, his voice slow and dull, almost a monotone.

'You know how easy it would be to take a taxi, or a train, or even to walk half a mile and make the visit you promised years ago, knowing that, if you simply turned up on the doorstep unannounced, you would be welcome. It would take an hour or two, no more, and you know, in your heart, that you ought to go, that you have neglected this friend, who has shown you nothing but kindness. You are almost certain he will be at home: he's old now, and you'd heard somewhere that he was ill. When you consider the alternatives – a café on the Plaza Mayor, a couple of hours browsing in the bookshops on Calle Agua – you know there is no reason not to go, no excuse for avoiding this small chore, which will give him so much pleasure. True, you have lost touch, and the last time you met, this friend was a little tedious, preoccupied with his health, or his daughter's recent divorce. Or he bored you with endless photographs of his grandchildren. Or perhaps you were annoyed by an impression you had, something quite fleeting and probably exaggerated, that this friend, who had once seemed so positive, so life-affirming, even, had become embittered, or narrow-minded. You tell yourself that you have moved on, that it's always wrong to go back, but you're dogged by guilt none the less. Finally, you decide to go – and now you are even more irritated by the existence of this friend. Now, you remember the disappointment you felt, the last time you visited, or you dredge from your memory an imagined betrayal. By the time you have reached the suburbs, you are already beginning to forget the name of his street, and later, as you skirt the edge of the park, you come to a standstill. It's warm; the sun is shining. Surely, you tell yourself, the city has never looked so beautiful, the lime trees by the zoo are just coming into flower, children are calling to one another in the middle distance. As you pass the café, the scent of fresh coffee and newly baked pastry draws you in. All you want is to be alone for a while, to sit quietly in the open air, watching the world go by. It's a moment of unadulterated pleasure. When you decide to abandon your search, you experience a moment of self-affirmation. Or rather, it's more than an affirmation of self, it's an accord with the whole of life, a celebration of being – an affirmation, yes, of pure being, in opposition to everything that is contingent. You feel at home in the world, you feel that, no matter where you are, you belong. The sensation lasts for minutes, perhaps longer, and you want it to stay for ever. But then – and you have no idea what prompts you to remember the friend you have abandoned – then, suddenly, the guilt returns. You imagine your friend will appear at any moment, and catch you out. Perhaps he has already seen you; perhaps he is watching, even now, as you sip your coffee in the afternoon sunlight. Yet even as this image returns to haunt you, you are aware of something else, a sensation you never expected. Now, for the first time, you realise that betrayal is a pleasure. To move on, to discard, to abandon, is essential to your notion of yourself. And then you see there is something more – something quite terrible. For, rather than give up this slender moment of pleasure, you know you would betray your friend totally, you would even kill him if need be. From this unimportant event – this imagined betrayal, this imagined murder – your mind follows a hopelessly logical path.'

Gold paused. Robert turned to look at him and saw that his eyes were shining, dark and bright, in the dim light of the bar.

'We have such banal expectations,' Gold murmured. 'Yet the logic is there. All you need do is follow that path.'

'To where?' Robert felt a bitter, resentful curiosity, in spite of himself. 'Why are you telling me this?'

'Freedom,' Gold said, simply; then added, after a few seconds, 'the freedom to be. Which you see is the opposite, the exact polar opposite of everything other people want from you, other people's – expectations. Freedom is the domain of monsters. To be free, you have to become a monster for others. Once you realise that, once you commit one entirely gratuitous act, your whole life is purged of those expectations.'

The man smiled.

'That girl over there,' he said. The insinuation had returned to his voice and Robert nodded, quickly, hoping the man wouldn't make a scene.

'What do you really want from her?'

Robert glanced guiltily across at the two women, who seemed entirely absorbed in their conversation.

'Nothing– '

Gold laughed, then stood quickly, and called the waiter. The girls looked round as the waiter sauntered across to the table, then the pretty one gave Robert an odd, quizzical look, before returning to her friend. Gold produced his wallet and handed the man a pile of bank-notes.

'Drinks for the house,' he said. The waiter looked puzzled, but took the bank-notes.

'Drinks for everyone,' Gold said slowly, spelling it out.

Robert jerked to his feet. 'I don't want anything,' he said. 'I have an appointment.' For a moment he thought Gold would force him to stay and he staggered sideways, stumbling over a chair, before he escaped into the blur of the street and the yellow-grey light of the evening.

For the next two days, Robert was alone. Sandra had decided she was ill and had taken to her bed with a vengeance; the only times Robert saw her was when he brought her water and fruit, which was all she would eat, and fresh supplies of books. The rest of the time, he wandered the streets or sat on the rocks; once, he saw the girl from the bar, walking alone in the plaza, and he stepped quickly into a sidestreet to avoid her. The fear of seeing Gold haunted him wherever he went, but he knew, if he did appear, it would be pointless trying to avoid him. If Gold didn't find him out when he chose, he would come at some other time and, once Sandra was well again, he might choose to make his next approach when she was there. Robert was terrified of this possibility, but he also realised that it wasn't only fear he experienced when he thought of Gold: there was a fascination, too, as if the man possessed a secret that Robert needed to understand, some hidden competence or way of being that set him apart from the rest of the world. It was an idea that had often occurred to him – an idea that there were people in the world who lived entirely by their own rules, their own vision. He had tried to convince himself that Gold was just some madman, one of those elaborate fantasists he'd read about, who were so convinced by their own mania, they had a purely artificial power over others – but he couldn't quite succeed. As the days passed, he began to imagine that Gold really was the killer of those women, and the thought that it might be so intrigued as much as it appalled him. On the third day, he picked up a copy of *Sur* in English. Another girl had been killed, a seventeen-year-old. Though few details were given, the suggestion of a slow, deliberate brutality was implicit in the article.

No sooner had he finished reading the piece, sitting in the warm sunshine outside El Nautico, than Gold appeared. He smiled as he approached the table. He was carrying the same English edition of *Sur*, folded neatly and tucked under his arm.

'Hello, again,' he said, as if he were simply another holiday-maker, meeting a fellow suburbanite from Croydon or Colchester and entering into that camaraderie that comes of being abroad –

a good excuse to lament the bizarre customs of the Spanish, the way they served hot milk with the tea at breakfast time, or their annoyingly loud conversations in cafés and bars. Robert nodded, almost imperceptibly, and put away his paper; the waiter, who looked no older than a schoolboy, came and took Gold's order, then they sat together in silence, like old acquaintances, with all the time in the world, till the young man returned, set down the coffee and disappeared.

Slowly, Gold unfolded his paper and laid it out on the table in front of Robert. It was open at a page of classified advertisements. Robert glanced at him.

'Look at this,' Gold said, stabbing at the page with his finger.

Despite himself, Robert began reading down the page. He was aware of Gold watching him, reading the adverts from the other side of the table.

— *Sandy, very sexy lady, blonde, blue eyes, 130 bust, playful body, full of vices. 24 hours, hotels, private visits.*
— **NEW**, *Cherry, bust 130, 1.80 hemispherical buttocks. Porno-fan, super sexy. Couples, visits, Greek. High-class, discreet. Elderly gentlemen also welcome.*
— *Maria. Andalusian beauty. Hot and sexy.* **I do what you like.**
— **WET AND WILLING!** *Hi, hot Sex-lover. Be happy you found 'Simply the Best' Sex-Service on the Coast. No lies, no fake promises, only the truth.*

Gold laughed.

'That's a good one,' he said. 'No fake promises!'

Robert sat back in his chair and decided to pretend the other man was invisible. Eventually, he told himself, Gold would give up on him and go away. He was afraid the stranger would see that he was flushed, that the advertisements had embarrassed and excited him. If he said nothing, Gold would recognise his mistake and leave.

Instead, Gold began talking quietly, telling him what he had done – how he had stayed in those rooms with his victims for hours, how sometimes they were too frightened even to struggle or cry out, how he did whatever he wanted, making it last so he could watch and listen to his victim, as her eyes pleaded for mercy, as she moaned through the gag he had forced into her mouth. He would have his camera with him, and he would take photographs. He told about how amused he had been, when he read in the papers that the killer saw his victims as animals, or objects – whereas for him, their humanity was the vital factor, the key to his pleasure, the whole point of his enterprise. It was essential to him, to think of these women as creatures of more than flesh and blood, exquisitely vulnerable, capable of real, conscious suffering. He would pause sometimes in his work to examine the contents of their rooms or apartments – the stuffed toys, the photographs, the clothes in the wardrobe. He would empty their handbags out on the floor and pick through the contents – there was always something there that touched or surprised him. The point was to remind himself of the victim's humanity, of her uniqueness.

Meanwhile, in a desperate attempt to block out Gold's voice, Robert closed his eyes and thought about autumn, about frost on the leaves and long streets in the suburbs and that feeling he would have when, on boyhood holidays, his aunt or someone would show him up to a narrow, musty room at the top of the house, with a walnut tallboy by the window and a crucifix over the bed, or a framed view of the harbour at Tobermory. He had felt safe in rooms like that, at a distance from everything, and all through the first evening he would imagine there was nothing to stop him locking the door and sitting there for ever, tucked up in bed, under clean sheets, reading the old copies of *Treasure Island* and the *Boys' Own Annual* that someone had left on the bedside table for him to find. Gold was still talking, but now Robert didn't understand what it was about, and he didn't want to understand. He sat as still as he could, waiting for the waiter to come and somehow rescue him from this madman, and he thought hard about those rooms, and winter, and morning frosts. Then he tried to imagine that town in Germany, the one with a river and an island, with five – or was it seven – bridges connecting the island to the surrounding land, a city famous for some problem in topology. Though he couldn't recall the name, Robert did remember the problem clearly: could a man walk the length and width of the town, crossing every bridge once, but never more than once? The answer to the problem was no, but for a long time nobody could prove it; he remembered reading about that town in a school text book, and trying to imagine it, in the winter time, as snow fell on the bridges and the streets, and that man wandered back and forth, retracing his steps, always returning to the same point and beginning again, for ever and ever. He liked to think of the gas lamps, and the snow falling on the dark water, and though he had never fully belonged to any place in his life, he knew that he belonged there, in that German town, whose name he could never recall.

'You're trying to convince yourself you don't believe it, aren't you?' Gold's voice was suddenly normal again, genuinely questioning, as if he were talking about the football, or some piece of news from home. Robert was surprised. If anything, the challenge had come just as he'd finally decided that Gold was entirely the monster he claimed to be.

'The monster has a function too,' Gold said, as if he had

read Robert's thought. He smiled wryly. 'That's the sad thing. Everyone has a part to play. Other people stay in their safe, polite world, and they watch for monsters. That's the only thing that keeps them honest. At least, they say, we're not the monster. As long as the monster exists, their tight little order means something.'

'You ought to see someone,' Robert ventured, desperately. He felt dizzy and breathless; he could scarcely believe he was sitting with this man in broad daylight, in the middle of the square, that he had somehow become visibly caught up in evil.

Gold laughed.

'I mean it,' Robert insisted. 'You ought to get help.'

Gold smiled again and shook his head.

'You don't mean it,' he said. 'You know as well as I do that there is no help.'

He turned then and gazed at Robert. There was a soft look in his eyes, a look of sadness, mingled with compassion.

'There's no help for either of us,' he said.

Robert looked away. He was afraid to move, afraid of what Gold might do if he didn't feel he had complete control of the situation.

'I don't know what you mean,' he said at last.

'Yes, you do,' Gold said. His voice was soft. 'You don't think I just chose you at random, do you?'

Robert jerked quickly to his feet, as if he had been struck. He couldn't tell if this easy remark, spoken in such a quiet, almost plaintive tone, was an immediate threat, or a kind of promise – and he couldn't tell which he feared more. At the same time, there was a sudden commotion, on the far side of the square. A couple of the carriage drivers were arguing with the hashish seller and another man, and now a policeman was approaching. Robert sat down again quickly, as if he were the one who ought not to be attracting attention to himself. At that moment, he half-believed the commotion on the far side of the square was nothing more than a diversion, a piece of theatre they had carefully staged so the police could move in and seize them both, the guilty and the innocent, indiscriminately. Gold laid his hand on Robert's arm, then he stood up. The trace of sadness had gone; he looked strong, almost radiant.

'Time to go,' he said. 'See you later.' Then he walked away quickly, in the direction of the sea front, without looking back.

That night, the Wednesday before they were due to leave, Robert sat for as long as he could in the pavement bar outside the hotel. Sandra was upstairs, having an early night; though she said she was feeling much better, she still hadn't left her bed for more than a couple of hours. By a slow process, she had become a kind of ghost in this place: she belonged to another world, another life, and there were times when Robert even forgot she existed. In a way, of course, she didn't exist. As far as he was concerned, she hadn't been real for years – and if a second honeymoon had any purpose at all, then perhaps it was only to demonstrate that fact. By the time he went to bed, at around midnight, he was drunk. He took the lift to the second floor and stood outside their room, listening. There was no sound. He opened the door and pushed it ajar. The room was dark and he could hear Sandra's soft, regular breathing. Quickly, silently, he pulled off his clothes and lay down. A moped rumbled past, just below the window; then blackness and silence hit him.

When he woke, Robert was convinced there was something in the room, something alive, like a bird or a lizard, a nexus of pulse and talons, fluttering against the wall in the far corner. He switched on the light, and immediately lost the sense of what he had imagined; he only knew he had been dreaming, and that, whatever the creature was, it had come from him. He was surprised and sickened for a moment by how real it had seemed, how intensely physical, then he picked up his watch from the bedside table. It was six fifteen; Sandra was still asleep. Through the half-open blind he could see that it was quite light, and he decided to go out immediately.

Even at that hour, there were people in the water: a couple, standing together in the shallows. He sat for a while on the bench, at the edge of the Balcon, and watched them: the man tall and thickset, with close-cropped, greying hair, standing in the wash of the tide, supporting the woman, who was much younger, and very slight. She lay almost motionless, floating slightly above the man's outstretched arms, totally confident, totally trusting, her face to the sky, her arms by her side. For some reason, Robert had a notion that she was blind, though there was no evidence to suggest it: apparently the man, who might have been her father, or even her grandfather, was teaching the girl to swim and, for their own reasons, they had chosen the cool of the early morning for their lesson. It was a perfectly innocent scene, yet, even as he watched them, Robert felt awkward and slightly ashamed, aware of an unsettling intimacy between the bathers, an intimacy upon which, even at this distance, he was intruding. Perhaps it was this, combined with the age difference, that had suggested to him that the girl was blind. She had placed her trust so firmly, so unshakeably, in the man, that she could happily close her eyes and let herself drift freely with the sway of the tide, confident that she would never come to any harm.

Robert spent the entire morning in the square. Occasionally, he bought a cold drink, but he couldn't even begin to think of eating, and the idea of going back to the hotel room filled him with an inexplicable dread. At the same time, however, as long as he didn't think about Sandra, or Gold, or the girl in the bar, he felt an odd peace, a sense of being outside himself, outside time and space, as long as he sat there, alone, in the quiet square. It was almost a pleasure, now, to watch the passers-by: the grotesque, the sad, the beautiful, the dying – they all looked like phantoms, evanescent and, at the same time, somehow contrived, like the characters in a puppet play. Around noon, as the church bells started up, a plump woman with a receding hairline and a large black mole above her left eye sat down on the bench opposite and began eating an ice-cream. Robert watched in fascination as she sucked the chocolate-coloured paste into her mouth, letting flakes of wafer spill over her tight black dress, completely intent on what she was doing. After a moment, her lips and chin, and even her cheeks, were smeared with the sticky, dark cream. Robert felt awkward: the pleasure the woman was taking in the ice-cream was so intense, so private, it almost offended him that she should indulge it there, in a public place, directly in front of the café where he was sitting. He tried looking away, but after a moment his gaze would return to the woman's face; fascinated, disgusted, he could barely take his eyes off her. It occurred to him that there was something obscene in her enjoyment, in the way she sat, her feet planted slightly apart, her hands moving all the time, turning her cone so the melting ice-cream would not drip over her clothes. She had the same unconcerned, unselfconscious air that cats have, when they set about their food, or when they find a comfortable place and begin grooming. At the same time, her actions had the quality of a performance, as if she was aware of being watched, and wanted to show she didn't care how she was perceived. When

104

she finished eating, she even licked her fingers, then took a handkerchief from her pocket and wiped her face.

Robert had become so absorbed in watching the woman that he didn't notice he had company until it was too late. All of a sudden, quietly, as if joining a friend who had been waiting for him, Gold had sat down at the table, so close that Robert could smell the man's aftershave. In panic, he looked around for the waiter, so he could pay and leave, but no one was there.

'Have you ever been walking in the Sierras?' Gold asked, without preamble, as if continuing a conversation that had been only momentarily interrupted.

Robert did not answer. Gold was no larger or heavier than he was, and he looked like any other British tourist, or possibly one of those residents who sit in the bars and cafés near the beach, reading the *Telegraph*, or the English-language edition of *Sur*. Yet Robert was afraid. He knew that this man was capable of anything, that he wouldn't care about making a scene, or even fighting in a public place. For all Robert knew he might even be armed.

'I have,' he continued, unruffled by the silence. 'You should go some time, on some hot afternoon in summer, when everyone else is indoors. Forget all that mad dogs and English-men stuff.'

He laid his hand on Robert's arm a moment, then withdrew it, softly.

'Go up into the hills, just outside some village somewhere. No need to go too far. Just enough to get away from the people, and out of sight of the houses. At first you think you'll find nothing there, just stones and lizards, and a few cats, ghosting out the heat in the shadows of a prickly pear. True, you have to look hard to see any more than that, but it's there. It flares up out of the dust, or it steps quietly out from the rocks and touches you

105

– and that's when you know what panic really is – not some sudden irrational fear, not fear at all, in fact, but an astonishing form of possession, a release from all concern, from all human limitation. You've been touched by a god, because that's what panic is – the god Pan. I know you don't entirely believe in this. Not yet. But you will. Because Pan exists; he's the only god there is, the only god that could ever be. You'll know that soon enough.'

Robert closed his eyes. He was trying hard not to listen, to think about something else. Suddenly, in that moment, he'd had the premonition of something, a flicker of agreement at some deep, unconscious level. Gold laughed.

'Don't be silly,' he said, as if he were talking to a child. 'You think something's going to happen to you, because that's how you were brought up, that's how you were trained to think. You can't see yet that you're just like me – but I see it, and Pan sees it too. That's why you're here. You've been wondering why you came – and soon you'll know. It's a terrible thing to be chosen, terrible and beautiful. But it doesn't matter, because it's also inevitable—'

He broke off suddenly. Robert opened his eyes and, following Gold's gaze across to the far side of the square, he saw a young woman who had just sat down on one of the benches, in the shade of a palm tree. The woman – who was little more than a girl, perhaps eighteen or even younger – was breathtakingly beautiful, in the Andalusian style, with large dark eyes, perfect, sand-coloured skin and thick black hair, bound in a coil around her head, so the long, fine neck remained visible. Her body was perfect, well-formed and slender, the legs, revealed by her short skirt, long and brown and unimaginably smooth, so that, in spite of Gold, Robert longed to touch her, to just lay his palm flat on her thigh, to feel the smoothness and the warmth.

'There – you see?' Gold continued, as soon as he knew he had Robert's attention. 'There's another one. Beautiful, isn't she?'

He gave Robert a sympathetic look, as if he were trying to let him know he could read his thoughts, then turned back to watch the girl. She had taken off one of her shoes, and was shaking it out. A trickle of sand spilled on to the flagstones.

'They're all the same,' Gold said, in a stage whisper. 'They all promise something – maybe pleasure, maybe love – something good and easy, whatever it is they think you want. It's all so natural – the most natural thing in the world. What they don't realise is that other promises can be made, and kept, without their even knowing.'

He smiled.

'It always surprises them,' he said. 'Always. And it's always such an exquisite pleasure, that surprise.'

He shook his head, as if in wonder. 'Once you've experienced it,' he said, 'you'll never exhaust its possibilities.'

Maybe it was his gaze, maybe it was the soft conviction in his voice, but suddenly, finally, Robert understood what he wanted. Now, for the first time – and the sensation was overwhelming – he realised that he had been chosen for something more than a confessor. At this, Gold smiled softly and nodded, encouraging him, as if he were working with a slow-witted pupil who has suddenly glimpsed the possibility of an answer to a problem in geometry or algebra – as if he only wanted Robert to know what he had to know, for his own good.

'Experienced what?' Robert asked, as the realisation grew.

Gold regarded him for a few seconds longer, then a flicker of sadness crossed his face and he stood up suddenly and turned back to the square. Robert thought, for a moment, he was about to do something, to make a scene, or perhaps call out to the girl, and he looked around desperately for help – but all Gold did was pat him gently on the shoulder, before he strolled off into the sunlit plaza, hands in his pockets, head in the air, looking for all the world like another innocent tourist. Even when he brushed past the young woman, who had risen from the bench and started across the plaza, it seemed almost accidental, the merest contact, which nobody but Robert would have noticed.

Some time in the middle of the afternoon, he found himself standing outside the police station. It was a perfect day: the people crossing the square and passing into the shade of the arches were sharp and focused, like the people in films; Robert had the impression that they were somehow special, selected from a range of possible passers-by: a tall, pretty girl in a bright yellow dress; a small, bright-featured boy in white shorts, standing by the ice-cream vendor's stand; an elderly man, in his best dark clothes, walking to Mass. As they passed him by, they appeared to be nothing more than extras; they were people with no inner life, no secrets; they existed for no other reason than to complete the scene, to make the town appear inhabited – and for this reason, they were safe, no harm would come to them, they would appear and disappear without mishap, without being touched in any way by fate. They were the kind of people who minded their own business, people who performed their parts and stepped out of frame, without attracting undue attention to themselves, as much a part of the furniture of the town as the buildings and the cars, and just as real.

Robert looked up at the windows of the police station. It could have been any municipal building – a health inspectorate, or a tourist bureau – and it was much smaller than Robert had imagined. Nobody here would speak English, of course; even if they did, they would misunderstand anything he told them – misunderstand or, worse, accuse him of lying, of wasting police time. Perhaps the police would decide that Robert was the criminal; perhaps they would even arrest him. He'd heard stories about police inefficiency and corruption, about men who had been falsely accused and thrown into jail for months, or even years, before they were finally released, without so much as an apology. His story was so unbelievable, they would automatically suspect him of some other motive, of some desire to obscure the truth, to cover his own misdeeds. After all, what evidence did he have? How could he prove this Gold even existed?

At that moment, as if the very thought had conjured the man out of thin air, Gold appeared. He was standing at the corner, next to the food stall; he must have been there for some time, for he was watching Robert with what appeared to be genuine curiosity. Seeing that Robert had noticed him, he smiled darkly, as if to say that he knew well enough why he was there: to say, moreover, that he knew what Robert was thinking, that he understood the reasons for his hesitation – understood them better, even, than Robert did himself – and it came as no surprise that Gold knew everything, that he had anticipated every nuance of self-doubt and absurdity that Robert was now experiencing. Why would a murderer confess his crimes to a complete stranger? And why would a man go to the police with such a story, unless he himself was implicated?

Gold watched him. The smile never left his face, but Robert could see he was watching closely, the way a doctor watches a patient, and he was certain the man could read his every thought. It was uncanny, the feeling he had, that he had just said something, moments before, said it aloud, so everyone could hear – and, now, all of a sudden, he was aware of being watched, not only by Gold, but by others, by those perfect passers-by as they glided through this movie of the town, and by a uniformed man who had just appeared in the doorway of the police station. A wave of panic surged through Robert's body, an unexpected and sickening moment of total fear, and he was convinced that he had spoken aloud, not only spoken, but blurted out everything, here, in the street – only in this version of events, he was the killer, he was the man who fitted all the descriptions, the one they had been hunting all those weeks. He looked over to where Gold had been standing, only a moment before, but nobody was there and, with a dizzying rush of horror, as he hurried away across the square, Robert felt himself abandoned, guilty beyond all doubt and incapable of defending himself against any charge they might bring against him.

The room was empty. Someone had come and made the bed, and the books that had been scattered around the floor had been stacked neatly on the table by the window, but there was no trace of Sandra. It was as if she had never existed. Suddenly, he was reminded of times when he was staying somewhere on business, or attending a convention, and of the pleasure he felt, when he came back to his hotel room and everything clicked back into place as soon as he was alone. That was the one thing he had always known for sure, the one thing he loved, that limbo of television and room service, which no one else could enter. He would slip the DO NOT DISTURB sign over the handle and close the door, then he would slide the bolt or click the deadlock. Alone. There were moments, laid out on the bed, listening to the quiet, when he understood what it meant to be real – not talking, not playing the game, but listening, breathing, thinking. A thought would form in his head, then another, and another still. He would remember the names of old classmates from school, the various cultivars in his father's apple orchard, the words to songs he hadn't heard in years. He would lie back and watch as the room dimmed; at moments like this, he would become aware of the film that was running in his mind, quite separate from his outward life, a film with its own plot, its own set of characters, a subtle interplay of clearly defined images and scenes. The film was bright and organic, more vivid than anything that ever happened in the daylight. Yet he knew, if he could have taken it out and projected it on a screen for his colleagues and friends, that it would mean nothing to them. It was like the photographs people carried in their handbags and wallets, photographs of wives and children, mothers and fathers, grandchildren and nephews: you showed them to someone else and immediately those rich presences were nothing more than faces, like the faces in the photo booths in bus stations and supermarkets – smiling, frozen, anonymous.

After a while, he had drifted off. He must have slept for some time, though he felt only moments had passed. When he woke, it was dark; he had the idea that someone else was in the room, but when he sat up and took stock of where he was, he realised he was still alone.

'Sandra?'

He knew she wasn't there, but he was aware of a sudden wave of fear and he had called out to dispel it, as if by saying his wife's name, he could draw her back to him. The fear had not entirely taken form, it was little more than the thought that, if Gold knew his name, he might also know about Sandra. He got to his feet quickly, went into the bathroom and splashed some cool water on his face; then, after changing his shirt, he hurried downstairs and out through the stone lobby, into the street.

It was the busy time of evening. People were gathering in the pavement café outside the hotel, or strolling up and down in twos and threes before dinner, tourists and natives, thin girls with mopeds, off-duty waiters going home to change for the night's fun. Robert looked around. He had half-expected to see Gold waiting for him on the corner; instead, he caught a glimpse of Sandra, with a pile of books in her arms, walking towards him through the crowd. She looked absent, yet contented enough, almost bovine; when he realised she had not seen him, he crossed the road quickly and dodged into a sidestreet. Minutes later, he was back in the bar with the hams and bullfight posters, at the same table as before, ordering a beer. All he needed, he knew, was a little space. Gold had unnerved him: it had all been some huge, sick joke, that story about the murders, a joke he had played on others perhaps, some inward sixth sense allowing him to select victims who might be lonely or vulnerable, and play on their imaginations. It was the first time Robert had thought of himself in that way, but it was the truth – a revelation, in fact – that years of confusion and loneliness, married to a woman he hardly knew, a woman he couldn't even touch, had left him vulnerable to people like Gold and to his own sick daydreams. Now, he told himself, as he sat gazing at the drink brimming in his glass, it was time for a change, time for a new life. A couple of drinks later, he had worked it all out. He would leave Sandra and quit his job. He would travel for a while, then he would decide what he wanted to do. There were all kinds of things he could do, if he put his mind to it. It was just a matter of deciding.

'Hello.'

He looked up. The blonde girl was standing beside him, her hand resting on the chair opposite. She seemed to be alone and Robert realised, for the first time, that he had hoped he would see her again. He noticed how perfect her hand looked, the nails beautifully rounded, the skin deeply tanned, then he looked her in the eyes. She was waiting for him to invite her to sit down.

'Hello,' he answered, feeling like an idiot.

'Are you on your own?' the girl asked.

'Yes.' Robert ventured a smile. His mouth felt tight and he realised that, on an empty stomach, the beers had gone to his head. 'Would you care to join me?' He almost laughed at himself, for sounding so formal.

The girl smiled and sat down. As if by magic, the waiter – an older man than her friend from the other night – appeared at the table, and they ordered more drinks. The girl seemed to have been drinking already: she told him her name was Marion, from Durham, as if she were a contestant on some game show, and Robert introduced himself. When the drinks arrived, there was a silence, while Robert cast around for something else to say, but he needn't have worried. In a practised, almost professional manner Marion began asking him questions, obviously to put him at ease, telling him things about herself that surprised him, odd irrelevant details, answers to questions he would never have thought of asking. It created a strange, sudden intimacy between them, and they ordered another round of drinks, and then another, till Robert lost count. Eventually, he had lost track of everything – the time, where he was, where he should have been – and he sat suspended in a vague, golden blur. By the time they left, he wasn't sure how, or even if, the girl had invited him back to her flat, he was just walking along a street with her, in the cool of the night, as if it was the most natural thing in the world.

The flat was small and untidy. The door gave on to a small sitting room, with no furniture other than a sofa and a coffee table, and there was a tiny kitchen – just a sink and a kettle, really – to one side. Robert sat down on the sofa, while Marion went into the kitchen to make coffee. She was talking about someone called Sam; Robert wasn't entirely sure who this person was, but he thought it was the woman he had seen her with in the bar, someone she worked with. He had lost track of the conversation when they'd reached the flat, and he'd been trying to decide whether to kiss her. As far as he had gathered, the girl worked as a courier, or a tour guide, and he thought Sam might have been her boss. Finally, he gave up wondering. He sat back on the sofa and watched her as she moved about the kitchen; then, aware that she had become aware of him watching her, looked around the little sitting room. There was a poster on one wall, some kind of Impressionist painting with poppies in an out-of-focus field and, in a row above the sofa, some crayon drawings, obviously done by a child. Robert stood up to take a closer look.

The drawings were remarkable. Each picture showed one or more figures, children and adults with black or straw-coloured hair and big, very blue eyes. The people were carefully drawn, and their clothes were detailed and brightly coloured but, as if as an afterthought, when the picture had been completed, every one of the figures was encased in a spiral of thin black lines, winding around and around each body like fine black wire. The effect was strangely beautiful and, at the same time, unexpectedly disturbing. Robert turned to Marion as she brought the coffee through.

'Who drew these?' he asked.

The girl looked uncomfortable. She handed him a coffee mug, then set hers down on the coffee table.

'My son,' she said. 'Andrew. He's four.'

Robert sat down beside her and placed his mug by hers. For a moment, he felt dizzy and scared, as he stared at her. His hands felt hard and cold all of a sudden, as if they were made of steel.

'Where is he?' he asked.

'He's at home,' Marion answered. 'My mother is looking after him.'

'Oh.'

Robert wanted to get up and rush out of the flat, before it was too late. In the bar, he had only wanted this woman – to come here, drink her coffee, kiss her, make love to her, then go. Now, for no good reason, he felt a wave of pity shiver through his flesh. He understood everything; he knew it, without a doubt. The story was too banal to even bother to think through. This pretty girl – blonde and tanned, carefree – was just another working mother, trying to keep things going, missing her son, who was far away, in a neat little semi in Durham with his grandmother. At the same time, he felt a ripple of anger pass through his body, an anger that was indivisible from the pity – and he realised, with a kind of slowed horror, that this was just what Gold felt, as he picked over his victims' possessions, a bright hard anger wrapped in useless pity, endlessly self-renewing, infinitely repeatable. He felt Marion's hand on his arm.

'Are you OK?' she asked.

He turned to look at her. In this light, she wasn't as pretty as she had seemed in the bar, when the first flush of drink was on him; she looked tired now, and her eyes were slightly red. Still, he felt a rush of automatic desire, like something inevitable, released by her touch, and he leaned forward to kiss her. She hesitated and, for a moment, he thought she was going to change her mind and tell him to stop; but she didn't, she just let him push her back, almost wearily, and he felt something dissolve in her body as she let him do what he wanted, some expectation, some thin, vague thread of *joie de vivre*, or hope, melting to nothing, under his clumsy hands.

When he got back, Sandra was in bed, lying on her side,

with her face turned towards the window, her back to the absence where he should have been. He listened a moment: her breathing was soft and regular and, deciding she must be asleep, he undressed quickly and slipped in beside her. He felt sick now. For a few anxious moments, he felt the pain rise in his chest, filling his throat, and he thought he would have to get up and go to the bathroom to vomit. Images of Marion filled his mind: she was tied up, with her mouth pressed against the floor, naked from the waist down, a thin film of blood on her lips and teeth. Or she was spread-eagled on the bed, face-down, and he was moving on top of her, holding a kitchen knife to her throat. He was amazed and sickened by the fact that these images excited him and he tried hard to put them out of his head, but the more he tried, the stronger they became. He tried thinking of something else. He thought of Sandra, asleep beside him; he thought about going back to work, then he remembered his plan – to quit, to leave Sandra, to run away from it all. Finally, he must have slept, for he found himself lying in a pool of warm water, the sunlight streaming through his closed eyes. He was swaying slightly with the motion of the tide as a school of tiny fishes – he could feel them, but he couldn't see – rose from the depths of the pool and began biting softly into his flesh, eating him away slowly, quietly, without pain. As they worked, gnawing him away, eating in towards the bone, Robert felt happy. It was good, he knew, that he would be gone soon; but when he woke, he was crying, noiselessly, the tears running into his hair and along his temples, crying for everyone – for the dead girls, for the woman with the ice-cream, for the hashish seller, for Marion, for Sandra, even for Gold. But most of all he was crying for himself, and for the notion he had taken for granted that, no

116

matter how cold it might be, there was a harbour somewhere, a place where he could rest, and think of himself as happy and free, and intrinsically, incontrovertibly, decent.

FOLIE À DEUX

When I can't sleep I get up and sit by the window, where I can see the sky. Sometimes there are stars and I try to remember the names of the constellations, but it's been a while now since Val was here, and he was the one who really knew all that stuff. I used to try staying in bed, telling myself I would fall asleep after a while, listening in the dark for his soft breathing, and the odd, small popping sounds he used to make with his lips when he was dreaming, though we hadn't slept in the same bed for years, not since we were small. It bothers me, thinking about him, and about how close we used to be. Now that he's gone, I have a tendency to brood: I fix on an idea and circle around it, over and over, never coming to a resolution, just lying in bed with my head buzzing. If I get up, I can at least sit by the window and look at the sky. It's a foolish thought, I know, because there's probably nothing in the world except the earth and the cold stars and the stones in the cemetery, but sometimes I think Val is out there, not in any one place, but just floating somehow, as if he was part of the whole universe, and not just the other half of me. When I think that, I come close to believing that everything is all right – what I'm looking for is a special thought, an idea that's almost there at the edge of my mind, a switch, almost, that I could throw, so that something in me would be turned off, maybe for ever. I don't want to die, or anything like that.

I don't miss Val, or not in the way people think. It's just that I know what their world contains, all the doctors and nurses and visitors, and I don't want it. I've had my life, really; I've had events. Now I just want some time to think.

When I do sleep, I almost always dream about Val. I had no idea our state of being – our state of grace – had a textbook name. *Folie à deux* is what they call it – shared insanity, madness times two. I never thought of it as a medical condition: Val and I had always been together; we were the two halves of something that, otherwise, would have been incomplete, and whenever I looked at him, I saw myself, perfectly reflected. Now they tell me it was a form of mania; they're saying he was inside my head all that time, and I wasn't thinking straight. That's why they parted us, the way teachers part troublesome children in school, so the weaker child can escape the bad influence. It's odd how they always assume the strong one is bad – or is it that they think the bad are strong? I don't know, but they're wrong about one thing. When they took him away from me, he died, and I went on living. No matter what they say, he couldn't live without me.

They can do whatever they like in the cause of justice, but as far as I was concerned, parting us was a kind of murder. They took away the one thing we knew for sure, the only identity we had. If they had been right – if I was the weaker one – I should have died years ago, and it's true that, when we were first parted, I missed Val terribly. It was like having a piece of my soul torn out by the root and thrown away. Now it's different. As long as he was still alive, I could imagine being together again, and I wanted that, from habit as much as anything else. But one day I realised he was dead – I don't know how, but I knew as surely as I've ever known anything in my life. They wouldn't confirm or deny it, and at first I was angry. I wanted to see him, to be sure. I know if I had died, Val would have wanted to look at my body: he would have been curious; it would be like seeing himself laid out in the coffin. He'd have wanted to touch the corpse, to lean in close and smell this dead version of his own flesh, identical in every respect to the body that still breathed. Surely they understood what it meant to me, to suspect that a part of myself had been taken away and sealed in a box, without my knowing for sure it was really gone. But they wouldn't talk about it, and I stopped asking. It was as if I had died too, and nothing mattered any more.

That was how Thomas must have felt, when Jesus was crucified. I remember how excited we were, when we read how Thomas was called 'the Twin' – nothing else was said, you just had to take it for granted that, if he was 'the Twin', then he must be Jesus' twin. That was why he couldn't believe Jesus had come back, unless he touched the wounds – or no, it wasn't that he couldn't believe, that was just how the witnesses saw it. They could never have understood why he had to touch the wounds, to slide his fingers into his brother's body, how he had always wanted to know what it was like, to be inside this identical other, not because he doubted his existence, but because he wanted to be him, for a single, dizzying moment. I remember the same feeling, when the priest came and told us about the soul. He seemed oddly sure of himself, oddly unquestioning, as he stood before us, moving his hands about in front of his body, as if he were performing some conjuring trick. It sounded as if he was describing a physical thing, something almost substantial, hidden in the body somewhere – a shadow on the thalamus, a stain between the liver and the heart. I knew that was wrong, because I knew, if I had a soul, it hovered somewhere between Val and me, a shared atmosphere, a rhythm that only worked when we were together. I couldn't have challenged the priest. I

123

couldn't say that I knew what was, for him, a matter of faith, was far subtler – too subtle to be considered, even; but he noticed my slight shake of the head, and he glanced from me to Val, and back, as if he had guessed what we were thinking. Then he went on, averting his eyes, the way a cat does when it wants to pretend you're not there.

After they parted us, I felt unreal, almost gaseous, unsure of myself. I became clumsy, I kept bumping into people, and knocking things over. Yet later, when I knew he was gone for good, I felt free for the first time in my life. My mind was like a wide, empty room, full of light and space. It wasn't like that before; it was like in music, when two melodies are going on at once – what do they call it? Counterpoint. I never felt I could tell my story, or even speak, because his voice was always there, entwined with mine, working against me. For years we existed without boundaries; our thoughts were seamless. Now I can say what really happened. I'm not suggesting it was all Val's fault: I just want to tell what I remember, to get it clear in my own mind. Maybe then I'll be able to wait for him in peace.

It was the warmest summer for years. I still remember how hot it was; the days merged, one into the next: a continuum of haze and birdsong. Most days, we went swimming. We despised the Lido and the public baths, and always chose the part of the river where it ran deep and quick, out beyond Broadburn Farm. Nobody else swam there, so we had the place to ourselves. We'd lie on the bank and listen to the cuckoo in the distance; in the evenings we'd see a fox wandering back and forth across the next field, scattering the rabbits. He didn't seem to be hunting so much as trapped in a maze of scent, following the hedge then faring out into the long grass, stopping now and then to listen and watch. Owls would come out to hunt before dark: we'd catch sight of them in the hedges, or floating over the fields, and once I saw one dip out of nowhere to catch a thrush in mid-air, as it flew from one bush to the next in the smoky twilight. In the heat of the afternoons, we'd swim in the deep water, where it was always cold: sometimes I would dive down and come up like a grebe, twenty yards away, and the cattle would lift their heads to look. They always seemed mildly surprised by my existence.

If we weren't out swimming, we'd go into town. I didn't like being there: the shops were crowded, and the people were hot and sweaty and ugly, picking things up and fingering them, leaving behind microscopic traces of minerals and dry skin. But Val would talk me into going: we'd wander from Boots to the Army and Navy, stealing things, just for the sake of it. We never took anything worthwhile: we only did it because Val enjoyed the risk. We'd go in once or twice a week and each time he'd steal something larger and more difficult to hide. Usually he threw away what he'd stolen. He didn't want the stuff. I could have accepted it if he'd only taken something useful.

One day I was keeping watch while he slipped a silver picture frame into his bag. It was by far the most expensive thing he'd ever taken, and I was planning to ask if I could keep it. It should have been a simple matter to take it and go without attracting attention – and it would have been too, but for Will Clark. I didn't see him till it was too late, but I could tell by the look on his face that he'd witnessed the whole thing. He didn't give us away – he just watched as we left the store, and I could see he was making a mental note of everything, to use it in evidence later.

When I told Val he got really angry.

'Why didn't you warn me?' he said.

'I didn't know,' I answered. 'By the time I saw him, it was too late.'

He looked at me in disbelief. Sometimes I tried not to know what he was thinking, but I always did, and he despised me for the pretence. I've read how there are tribespeople who believe the human soul is manifold. This is a common notion: rather than being a single entity, the spirit has a number of different aspects, which take up residence wherever they can: a pool of water, an earth formation, a totem creature that the child's father chooses on the day it is born, placing the afterbirth on a rock and calling the animal out, to snare its hunger. I read a story once, in a magazine, where a woman had created a garden in the grounds of a derelict house in New York City. Here and there, among the undergrowth, she had placed the toys and trinkets she had found abandoned on the streets: teddy bears and dolls, propped in the angles of the trees; a jack-a-lantern, grinning in the rain; mechanical clowns, wound down for ever, marooned among the weeds. In one of the pictures, the garden was peopled with pale, questioning faces, like the faces of lost children, or stylised ghosts. The accompanying text explained that the woman was homeless, an elective mute who devoted her entire life to the creation of this garden, walking the city for miles every day, searching for objects she could use in its decoration. Nobody knew why she was creating this special piece of ground. It could have been that she was building a shrine to the remembered dead, or trying to reassemble her own fragmented self from these random images – but then, she could just as easily have been wandering the streets, like so many others, gathering whatever she could find, choosing one thing and rejecting another, for no good reason, other than the desperate desire for something to do to pass the time.

It's hard to say why things happen: you read a story in a

magazine and suddenly you become aware of something you hadn't understood till then. Or else the picture is only a prompt, an alarm that brings to the surface something you had guessed was there all along – looking back you remember hints and glimpses, you realise, in fact, that it was staring you in the face all the time. Sometimes I couldn't tell Val's thoughts from my own: I would think something and he would do it, or I would think about something without knowing why, and it would only come to me later that it was him who was thinking, it was my brother whose being was so intertwined with mine that we shared our thoughts and our actions, that we could never escape from the bond that united us. At that moment, I knew we were deciding to kill Will – but I couldn't tell which of us it was who had initiated the idea, even if it was Val who did all the talking. I'm just as guilty – and just as innocent – as he was.

'What do you think he'll do?' I asked him.

'Will Clark?' he said, with exaggerated disgust. 'Will Clark is a creep. He'll tell somebody, that's for sure. I'm surprised he didn't say anything in the shop.'

I couldn't argue with him. Will was in our class at school – nobody liked him, and even the teachers kept him at a distance, no matter how much he sucked up to them.

'What are we going to do?' I asked.

I have to be sure about this. I have to be certain it was him, not me, who decided. I have to be certain he said it out loud, that he didn't just think it. If I remember him saying it then, at that moment, there could be other reasons than the most obvious one: I could be imagining it to explain what happened later, and so exonerate myself, because it would have been his idea, he would have been to blame, if he really had said, 'We'll have to shut him up, won't we?'

★   ★   ★

From that day on, we were obsessed. We planned everything to the smallest detail: Val would make friends with Will and invite him to come swimming one morning in our special place. He said Will wouldn't be able to refuse – he'd think we *liked* him all of a sudden, and he'd be grateful. He had to know how unpopular he was. Val would tell him to keep the whole thing a secret; he wasn't to let his parents know where he was going. When we had him in the river, we'd hold him under till he drowned. Will was always boasting about what a great swimmer he was, but even if that were true, he would be no match for the two of us. When he was dead, we would leave him there and go into town. Nobody would suspect we'd been anywhere near the river.

I was pretty sure it wouldn't work. Will would think we were just trying to get round him – but Val said that was all the more reason for him to come, because it would make him think we were scared. He'd imagine he had some power over us, because of what he'd seen – and as it happened, the plan worked. Val did a real job on Will, as far as I could tell, and it wasn't long before the date was set.

I didn't believe we would really go through with it, though. I went along with the plan, thinking we were just going to give him a fright, so he wouldn't tell about the shoplifting. Of course, I should have known I was only fooling myself. Nobody knew Val better than I did. Once he had an idea in his head, nothing I could have said or done would have changed his mind.

We went to meet Will on a Wednesday, in the middle of the holidays. It was one of those soft, damp mornings, when the sun takes a while to cut through the haze. We didn't wait for Will: I undressed quickly and slipped into the cold water, and Val followed, gliding away from me immediately and vanishing into the blackness under the willows. He loved it there: he said he could feel drowned bodies shifting in the water, brushing his skin with their bruised fingers. I told him that was the riverweed, but he just laughed.

'Believe what you like,' he said. 'You're entitled to your opinion.'

But I couldn't believe what I liked. I couldn't do anything he didn't want to do; I couldn't even tell his thoughts from my own. My existence was so tangled up with his that we shared everything. We even had the same dreams. Now they say that he was the guiding force and any power I had was his, not mine – yet when I swam into the deep water, where the weeds grew, I couldn't help feeling those fingers, brushing my arms and thighs, and sometimes I could see the blue faces, staring up at me through the water. I couldn't believe they were sad there; it seemed so perfect an eternity, to lie in the cold river, under the summer heat, letting the current flow through their dreaming minds.

When Will arrived, half an hour late, he didn't see us. I watched him, standing on the bank, looking downriver; then Val called out and he turned quickly, smiling, too obviously friendly to be trusted.

'There you are,' he said.

'Here we are,' Val answered, swimming towards him. 'Come on in. The water's icy.'

Will looked around hesitantly. For a moment I thought he'd turn and run, but he smiled when Val appeared in the pale sunlight and stood up, brushing the water off his face with the palm of his hand.

'We thought you weren't coming,' Val said.

Will apologised. I was quite surprised that he could act so well, knowing what he knew, but then Val was acting too, and Will had no idea what he intended. He put on his swimsuit – an oddly glossy thing – and lowered himself gingerly into the water.

'It *is* cold,' he said.

'You'll soon warm up, once you get going,' Val answered, striking out for the deep current midstream.

Will followed gamely. I felt a stab of pity, that he didn't suspect us, but at the same time, I couldn't see any way out of the plan. I couldn't let my brother down, just to save this fool. He kept his head above water all the time – it was obvious he wasn't the swimmer he pretended to be – and he had this self-conscious look on his face, as if he was being watched, as if the whole world was waiting to pass judgment on him. People don't understand that they're not always the centre of attention. They don't see that others have their own concerns. The way Will acted annoyed me, to tell the truth, and when Val gave me that look, to say it was time, I realised it didn't actually matter whether Will lived or died. I think if I'd been on land, I might have felt differently, but there, in the dark water, I couldn't care less. Val gave the signal and dived down: the last I saw of Will, he was looking confused – maybe he'd felt something pass between us, but he didn't know what, and by then it was too late. He didn't stand a chance in the deep water. A moment later he disappeared and I dived under. I don't really know what happened then – I caught hold of his arm and pulled him down, and he struggled for what seemed a long time, though it was probably no more than a few minutes. When he stopped moving, we let him go. He shifted away in the water, and I came up, into the light. Val was grinning.

'Well?'

I couldn't speak. I just nodded.

'Easy peasy,' he said, splashing a handful of water in my face and kicking away towards the bank.

★   ★   ★

It wasn't as easy as he'd thought. We'd made one mistake after another. Will had told just about everybody he was going swimming with us that day, but we denied ever seeing him when we were questioned. Then there were the bruises on his arms. It turned out the police knew right away that he hadn't drowned by accident: there were all kinds of clues that pointed to us, but we stuck to our story, even when we should have known the game was up. Val said you could get away with just about anything, if you didn't waver: the police were idiots, all we had to do was brazen it out. But in real life the police aren't stupid, and I had to admire the way they caught us out at every turn. It was fascinating to watch as the case against us grew, till even Val knew in his heart that it was hopeless. They were so sure of themselves, I started to believe they had a witness, someone who'd seen the whole thing. I found out later there was nobody, but by then it was far too late.

The press really took to Val. They cast him as an evil, Svengali figure, a child-sadist who didn't know the meaning of remorse, but they still couldn't get enough of him. As far as they were concerned, I was just his puppet, and I didn't get half the coverage he got. Not that I'm complaining – it helped to have people feeling sorry for me. As long as he lived, Val would never be free. On the other hand, I could be out in a few years.

Ever since it came to me that he was dead, I've tried to believe in a vague, cinematic form of transmigration – and I've almost succeeded. I almost imagine him passing through a wave of static, or sitting in a room somewhere, some branch-line waiting room with a hint of Christmas about it, where people come and go all day in old-fashioned winter coats, the men in hats and leather gloves, the women in headscarves, entering quietly, leaving trails of snow and dead leaves on the oakwood floor, bringing that scent of ozone and grass that lingers a while before it fades, just as the people fade, then arrive elsewhere. For us, reincarnation would surely be simple, like the conjuring tricks we used to practise when we were children. But in the end, it didn't work: even when I knew he was dead, the possibility of his being somewhere else, in another body, remained an abstraction. He couldn't exist without me, you see, and I only exist without him in a kind of limbo, an eternal summer of my own, where I watch and wait, free of identity, beyond all human jurisdiction.

KATE'S GARDEN

The day Tom Williams came back I was still working at home. The good thing about freelancing was that I got to be alone all day, in an empty suburb, just me and the cats and the blackbirds, and an occasional heron, standing motionless in the reeds, down by the river. I liked that feeling: I never tired of raising my head, halfway through a piece of work, and noticing the light at the window, the still gardens, the empty gravel paths and lawns. It was a world where nothing had ever happened. Time had passed – I would know by glancing over at the clock on the mantelpiece – but the movement had been so fine it was imperceptible. On those warm spring mornings, I kept having privileged glimpses into limbo: a state, not of suspension, but of infinite potential.

My study was upstairs at the back of the house. I'd placed the table so I could see the Williams's garden, rather than my own: ever since Tom had left, eighteen months before, Kate had worked out there every weekend, digging, planting, weeding, pruning, sowing. She was a fine gardener, with an excellent eye for colour and texture, and what had been an attractive plot before Tom disappeared was now a work of art. Kate was a slight woman, pretty and nervy, with tiny birdlike hands, but she extended the patio herself, and she carried large, soggy bags of mulch or compost from the front yard, where the delivery men left them, and dug them in herself, working through every

135

Saturday afternoon and all day Sunday, intent on what she was doing, single-minded, utterly absorbed. I think, for the first time in her life, she was truly happy. Making that garden may have been her therapy, but it was also her joy.

On weekdays, I got to admire her handiwork. The other gardens could look odd, sometimes, for being deserted all day: I had a sense, occasionally, of something missing there, but Kate's garden was all the more beautiful when she wasn't in it. It was as she intended, I think: a home for the plants she'd chosen and nurtured; a refuge for birds and hedgehogs; a breeding pool for frogs; a lure, in the early morning, for hungry deer. The only sign that the garden was meant for human use was an old wooden bench that she scrubbed and oiled every spring, and put away in the shed in October. There was no lawn, no drying area, no barbecue. Instead, she filled the space with lilies, junipers, irises. She had rare alpines and a rose-covered trellis to hide the shed. At the centre of one flower bed, she had placed a large, amphora-shaped pot. I waited weeks to see what she would plant in it, thinking it was rather beautiful as it was, standing empty, filling with light and rain. It was some time before I understood that that was exactly what she intended.

It's no exaggeration to say that Tom disappeared. In some ways, it was no surprise, either. Tom was a strange man. I remember, when we first moved in, Kate came round to introduce herself and invited us to dinner. All through the meal, Tom barely uttered a word, keeping himself busy with passing plates and serving bowls, clearing up between courses, or opening bottles of wine. Kate ignored this pantomime: the conversation rolled along naturally without Tom's participation, ranging from where to buy furniture through gardening tips to what I was working on at that moment. Then, halfway through the sweet course, the talk came round to an article about twins that Janice had read in a magazine, about how twin births occur more often than is generally known, but one of the twins is absorbed by the other, or dies, in the womb. Tom listened intently.

'I should have been a twin,' he said, when Janice had finished.

My wife turned and gave him her best interested look.

'Really?'

'Yes,' Tom said, softly. 'I don't have evidence, nobody ever told me, but I know it's true. I had a twin once: maybe he died, maybe he's hidden inside me – I don't know what happened to him, but I know he existed.'

I glanced at Kate. She was staring out of the window at the darkening garden.

'But how do you know?' asked Janice.

Tom shook his head softly and gazed at her. For a moment I thought he was going to cry.

'Because I miss him,' he said.

He smiled immediately, sensing he had taken the conversation too far.

'Anyway,' he continued, 'I've always thought there ought to be someone else like me in the world. Someone who sees things from my point of view.'

He smiled again, to let us know he was only joking, and offered Janice more cream; then, after an awkward silence, Kate asked Janice something about her work, and the conversation continued as before.

Tom barely spoke another word for the rest of the evening.

For a time, we had the usual neighbours' arrangement with the Williamses. We took turns issuing invitations for dinner, about once a month, always leaving a loophole for excuses. Then, one late summer afternoon, Tom went out in his shirt-sleeves and never came home. Kate called the police, then the hospital; she wrote to Tom's sister in Jersey. There was no sign of him. It was as if he had vanished off the face of the earth. I don't know what I would have done next, but it seemed to me that Kate gave up too easily. I could imagine searching for Janice for ever, if the same thing had happened to us. But Kate seemed almost relieved. She kept going to work – she only had one day off in those first few weeks of Tom's absence – and she spent the weekends in her garden; whenever I saw her, she greeted me as if she hadn't a care in the world. She seemed so contented, I was too embarrassed to ask if there was any news of Tom.

I could never imagine being with anyone but Janice; I could never imagine wanting anyone else as I have sometimes wanted her, with the sheer vivid physicality of desire that grips me unexpectedly, even now, when I watch her applying her lipstick or fixing her hair in the mirror, or when she comes in from the bathroom, wrapped in a clean towel, with drops of water still glistening on her shoulders. I could never imagine feeling for anyone else what I feel for my wife, yet I think I fell in love with Kate Williams a little, during that first year when she was living alone. It was something about the clothes she wore: the green duffel coat, the red and cream tartan scarf, the black woollen hat that she kept pulling down so it almost covered her eyes. I would catch myself wandering out into the garden for no reason on a Sunday afternoon, just so I could talk to her. I can't explain the sensation I had, when she put aside her rake, or hand fork, and stood chatting to me, her hands moving all the while. I was fascinated by her hands. She never wore gloves, so her fingers would usually be crusted with soil, or scratched in places where she'd caught herself on a briar or a thorn. It wasn't desire I felt, but it wasn't only compassion; it was a pure, dizzying love. Sometimes when I went back inside, after talking for a while, Janice would look at me strangely.

'What is it?' she'd ask, as if she'd read some unexpected tenderness, some unwarranted concern in my face – even though I knew my expression was quite noncommittal.

'Nothing,' I would answer, casually.

'Were you talking to Kate?'

'Yes.'

'Ah.' She would pause a moment. 'How is she?'

'Fine, I think.'

'Any news of Tom?'

'I didn't ask.'

There would be another short silence then, so it would seem she was thinking of what she was about to say next for the first time.

'We ought to invite her over,' she would say, and I would agree immediately. We would tell ourselves it was the least we could do, we would look at our diaries later and set a date and have her round, for dinner, or a drink. Then we would forget all about it. For different reasons, neither of us wanted her in our house. She made us feel awkward for being together, even though she seemed happy by herself. It was an assumption we made, based on our own lives, that any woman whose husband had left her must be lonely under the brave façade she maintained for the rest of the world. Or maybe it was an assumption Janice made, an assumption I was obliged to share. I wasn't altogether sure what Kate felt but, though she had never once talked about it, and even though she hadn't much liked him, Janice was certain, deep down, that Kate was waiting for Tom to come home.

★   ★   ★

139

I had been working all morning. The book I had just begun translating was well-written and engaging, a literary biography of the poet George Seferis. It was the culmination of a lifetime's study, really a labour of love, and I felt privileged to be working on it. I had been utterly engrossed for some time: I might never have noticed Tom if I hadn't heard a flutter of wings and looked up. A bird had almost flown in through the open window, then veered away at the last moment. I barely saw it but, looking down into the sunlit rectangle of Kate's garden, I saw Tom quite clearly, sitting upright, with his arms folded, on the dark wooden bench. He looked much as he had the day he left: his hair was a little longer, but he was wearing what looked like the same white shirt, the same light-green trousers, the same boots. It had been almost two years; now, here he was, sitting quietly in the garden, as if he'd just stepped out to take the sun. I could scarcely believe it. He looked too substantial to be a ghost or an apparition yet, at the same time, there was something unreal about his being there, in the ordinary daylight. It took a few moments for me to work out what it was about him that looked out of place, but when I did I understood how much he had changed.

The kind of people I know usually dismiss any talk of auras as mystical mumbo-jumbo, but I don't think there's anything supernatural in it. Every human body gives off a light of some kind. There are days when Janice is perfectly golden; she's someone who attracts light and adds to it a touch of her own, buttermilk-yellow warmth. Other people are subtler, or more subdued: they reflect greens or blues or crimsons, depending on their mood, on how happy or tired they are. That morning, when I saw Tom sitting in his wife's garden, he was wrapped in blackness – only it was more than that, there was a kind of luminescence to his body, what I can only describe now, remembering it, as a black light. I had never seen it in him until that moment; yet, at that moment, I knew I had always suspected it was there. I've never seen it in anyone else. It was the only time I have ever encountered a tragic figure, and I knew, without hearing his story, that tragedy had somehow overtaken him, either on the day he disappeared, or some time later, when he was lost and trying to find his way home.

I couldn't be completely sure, but I guessed he hadn't seen me. He seemed not to see anything; he simply sat stock still, with his arms folded over his chest, gazing straight ahead. I could have left him there; I could have gone back to work and pretended I hadn't noticed him. It was none of my business, after all. It wasn't as if I'd ever liked him much. As far as I was concerned, he was a bit of an oddball, a man who had casually walked out on his wife, without a word of explanation, without even a postcard to let her know if he was alive or dead.

I could have left him out there, but I didn't. I assumed he'd gone away without a key to the house, and he was waiting now, for Kate to come home and let him in. He must have known he'd have a long wait. It was a warm morning, but I wasn't sure it was warm enough for him to sit out there all day in his shirt-sleeves. I'm not sure if any of this is what I was thinking at the time, though. In the end, it was probably curiosity that made me ask him in. Or perhaps it was something more. Perhaps I was already harbouring the suspicion that what had happened to Tom and Kate could happen to anyone: that any love affair, any marriage, however passionate, however satisfying, was an invention of sorts, part good luck, part imagination. I knew, at the back of my mind, that there were times when I had to work to keep my idea of Janice intact. If that was the case, there would be times when she had to work just as hard. At one level, it was really nothing more than a conjuring trick and I was already wondering what it would take to break the spell. Perhaps that was what passed through my mind, as I walked downstairs and opened the back door, to ask Tom inside.

He didn't respond at first. He looked up and stared at me for a long, unsettling moment; I'm pretty certain he didn't recognise me: he'd forgotten who I was and, from the look on his face, I could tell I wasn't all he had forgotten.

'Would you like a cup of coffee?' I called over, in as matter-of-fact a voice as I could manage.

He stared at me in silence for a few moments longer, then shook his head.

'It's no trouble,' I said. 'Kate won't be home till later. You might as well come in for a while.'

All of a sudden, without my knowing why, I felt it was important that he come in. It had never occurred to me before, but at that moment, I was aware of a kinship between us, a likeness. Perhaps he was aware of it too; or perhaps he only responded out of politeness, or sheer passivity, but he stood up then, and walked over to the fence that divided the two gardens. He looked puzzled, as if he hadn't expected to find a barrier, though the fence had always been there.

'Come around the front,' I said, quietly. 'I'll put the kettle on.'

When I remember that day, I think of Tom as a ghost, a phantom who sat silently at my kitchen table, and drank three cups of coffee, one after another, like a man dying of thirst. I made small-talk for a while, and he listened, with his eyes averted, nodding or shaking his head from time to time, or making small, unintelligible sounds. I talked about myself, about Janice, about people in the village, but for some time I didn't mention Kate, and I didn't ask the one question he must have known I wanted to ask more than anything. It was odd. I had to know why he had left – it wasn't my business, but it didn't really matter, one way or another. He could answer, or he could simply refuse to speak. I had nothing to lose by speaking out. Finally, I gave in to the impulse – to the real need to understand what had driven him away.

'What happened to you, Tom?' I asked him. I was aware of how quiet my voice was, of how gentle I had managed to sound. He looked up at me: he seemed quite mystified, as if he hadn't understood the question. Then, after a long pause, he sighed and shook his head.

'Nothing happened,' he answered, just as quietly. 'Well, nothing I could tell you about. I just went for a walk that day, and realised I couldn't go home. It wasn't right any more. It wasn't fair on Kate.'

'It wasn't very fair to go off without even letting her know where you were,' I replied, a little more sharply than I had intended.

He gazed at me. He seemed stunned, and I realised, even before he spoke, that Kate had lied to us – by omission, no doubt, but intentionally, nevertheless.

'Did Kate tell you that?' Tom asked.

'Well,' I said, in as conciliatory a tone as I could manage, 'not in so many words. I suppose we just assumed.'

He nodded.

'Of course.' He spoke as quietly as ever, but there was bitterness in his voice.

'I telephoned her,' he said. 'And I wrote, four times. I couldn't tell her where I was, but I wanted her to know I was all right.'

He set his cup aside and stood up.

'I'll be going now,' he said. 'Thanks for the coffee.'

I stood up too.

'Kate won't be back for hours,' I said. 'You can stay here if you like. I'll just be upstairs. Make some coffee. Keep warm.'

He smiled slightly.

'That's kind of you,' he said, 'but I'm not waiting for Kate.'

He moved towards the door.

'Then why did you come?' I asked.

'I was happy here,' he replied. 'That was a long time ago, but I still think about it.'

I didn't speak. I couldn't think of anything to say and, for a moment, I thought he was on the point of telling me his story after all. Then the moment passed and I knew he would never tell anyone why he had left, not even his wife. He couldn't.

'The garden looks nice, don't you think?' he said.

I nodded.

'It's beautiful.'

He looked down at his feet and I thought he was about to cry.

'I just wanted to see,' he said at last. He smiled again and made his way through the hall to the front door and stood waiting for me to open it, to let him go back into the nothing from which he had come.

'Where will you go?' I asked.

He shook his head slightly.

'I don't know,' he said. 'Anyway. Thanks.'

He made a slight gesture that made me think he wanted to shake hands, but before I could respond, he turned and walked away, a man in his shirt-sleeves, out for a walk in the empty suburbs.

A few nights later, I couldn't sleep. I decided to get up and work for a while: it's something I do from time to time, to get me through the insomniac hours. I work well at night, and I enjoy being alone, listening to the owls as they flit back and forth along the riverbank. I had gone through to the study, as usual, to avoid disturbing Janice but, before I could switch on the lamp, I caught a glimpse of white, moving in the dark, beneath our apple tree. It was only the ghost of a movement and, when I looked again, there was nothing; yet I was sure, without knowing why, that Tom was there. It was an absurd idea: even Tom couldn't disappear like that, in a single movement, melting into the darkness, crossing back into the limbo to which he now belonged. Yet I was convinced that he had returned, as a ghost returns, for one more look at the garden his wife had made.

I didn't tell Janice that Tom had been in our kitchen and, of course, I didn't mention his late-night visit. I didn't say anything to Kate, either. There was no point. Tom had come home for his own reasons, and now he was gone. Kate continued in her garden and I still admired her handiwork, but only from a distance. I no longer invented excuses to go out and speak to her; I think she must have noticed the change, but she didn't seem bothered by it. She was happy that Tom had gone. There was something offensive about that happiness, but I didn't want to spoil it by telling her what I knew.

Yet perhaps there was another reason why I didn't want to talk about Tom's visits. I'm still not quite sure what I felt then, or how I feel now, but to speak at all would have been something like an admission of guilt, of thinking the wrong thing and so putting my faith in danger. It would have meant admitting to my suspicion that love is an act of faith. It may come by chance, it may begin as something else, but it continues only by a deliberate and sustained effort; it doesn't endure of itself, it has to be maintained, by strength of will and the force of imagination. I wasn't sure what Janice believed, but I had no intention of tempting providence by discussing Tom, or Kate, or how fragile I knew our lives were. We could grow apart, or we could take one another for granted; we might meet other people and drift into something easy and fleeting; I could look up from a newspaper some spring morning and find myself gazing at a stranger. If we had ever stopped to think, we might have seen all the possibilities. Part of the game we were playing, part of the act we had to sustain, was pretending the danger wasn't there. As far as we were concerned, we believed we would exist for ever in that house; we would never die, or if we did, we would vanish together, without a sound, leaving no trace behind. That was the superstition by which we lived: what we didn't recognise wouldn't find us. We assumed the bad things would happen to other people and went on living, with our eyes averted, moving from one day to the next, with no obvious purpose; but all that time, in complete secrecy, we were working to maintain the fiction we had to believe, in order to carry on.

FINDERS KEEPERS

It was just like Stewart to pick the runt of the litter. In those days, he had a gift for it; everything he owned was defective in some way: the watch that kept stopping, the incomplete jigsaws and board games he'd buy at church fêtes and jumble sales. The puppy he'd picked out was a male, but he insisted on calling it Lassie, like the dog in the films. As soon as it was grown, it started wandering off, though it always came home when it was hungry. It would turn up at the back door and wait there till Stewart came out, then it would jump all over him, licking his face and barking, wild with gratitude, as if relieved to have escaped some unexpected abandonment. Stewart loved that dog – the uglier it got, the more unpredictably it behaved, the more he loved it, and I was obliged to love it too, or he made me feel I was guilty of some deliberate betrayal.

So that summer, when Lassie ran off and didn't return – not that day, or the next, or the day after that – the whole family had to be worried. We let it go for as long as we could, then Dad went through the pantomime of telephoning the police, providing a detailed description of the missing animal to the speaking clock, or some mystified operator at the other end of the line. Mum said she was sure Lassie would turn up, but after a few days we all began to think the worst. The following Saturday, at about six in the morning, I found Stewart in the kitchen, waiting for me.

'You're up early,' I said.

'I've had breakfast,' he replied, as he started towards the door. 'Can I go out?'

'Where?' I asked.

'To look for Lassie.'

My heart sank, because I knew I would have to go with him. That was why he'd waited, of course. He'd set me up. I usually went fishing on Saturdays. Sometimes I took Stewart, but mostly I went on my own. I liked having that time to myself, to sit by the water, watching the river flow. I think I knew I was in the process of losing something – the map in my head was changing, significant landmarks were beginning to fade – and I was trying to hold on for a while to a boy's life. Maybe I wasn't fully conscious of the fact, but at some level I was aware of what was happening. Those summer days on the riverbank were precious to me – but if Stewart went looking for Lassie, I'd have to go with him. If the dog had been hit by a car, it was probably lying in a ditch somewhere; if it had fallen into a borehole, Old Mr Bremner might have found it, and I wasn't sure what he would do with a dead dog. He'd probably bury it, but you couldn't be sure: Old Mr Bremner was a strange man. At one time, I used to go out to the derelict kilns on the other side of his farm, to be on my own for a while. The place was a ruin, even then: it was tucked away at the edge of his land, half-hidden by shelterbelt. When I climbed the fence and passed from the sunlit field into the cool shade of the trees, I felt I was crossing a border into limbo, country that was at once mysterious and familiar, immersed in an almost tangible silence, the outer limits of a secret world. Occasionally I'd find rats or crows tied upside-down in the hedge with baling twine;

it seemed to me they were intended as markers, to show the boundaries I shouldn't cross – the beginning of Old Bremner's domain. I felt like a trespasser, but I'd still go out there and sit in the shade, listening to the birds, or the silence. Sometimes I'd take a cigarette I'd stolen from my father's pack of Capstan Navy Strength, and I'd climb up into a gap in the wall and sit there, hidden, watching the smoke drift in the shadows. One afternoon I clambered on to the broken rooftop and, with my arms spread out like a tightrope artist, I started walking across. I almost made it, but a few feet from the end, I got complacent and crashed into a patch of nettles fifteen feet below. It was Old Mr Bremner who found me: he came by, carrying a gun, about ten minutes later. At first I thought he'd come to shoot me for trespassing on his land, but he just took one look at the way I was lying, nodded, and walked off back to his farm to fetch help. He didn't say a word. I'd broken my leg and he'd been able to tell just by looking. It was a couple of months before I got to walk again, but as soon as I could, Mum insisted I go out there to thank him for his help – and I did: I knocked at his door for a long time, but even though I knew he was there, he didn't answer. When I got home, Mum said not to worry, Mr Bremner just wanted to be left alone, and it was best not to bother him again.

It was a warm morning. A heavy dew had fallen overnight, now steam was rising from the walls and fences on Station Road and the lawns in front of the neat low houses sparkled in the sunlight. There had been an accident at the corner of King Street – the road was strewn with tiny chunks of windscreen glass, spotted here and there with fragments of orange and crimson from the indicators. I looked at Stewart: he seemed not to have made any connection between Lassie and the debris on the road and

I realised he wasn't looking for that kind of evidence. To keep him distracted, I led him out along Fulford Road, skirting the edge of the Bremner farm, heading for the old kilns. I didn't want him to go looking in places where there was any chance of finding Lassie dead. After the kilns, I'd suggest we split up for a while, so I could check the boreholes while he was occupied with something else.

I hadn't been to the kilns since I broke my leg. It was more ramshackle than I remembered: most of the staircase had fallen away, and some of the walls had collapsed inwards. The inside was littered with old newspapers and broken glass; in one corner, someone had abandoned a half-eaten take-away and it was crawling with maggots now, small and white and moist, as if the rice grains had come to life. We found a dead bird floating in the water at the bottom of one of the pits, but there was no sign of Lassie. Stewart looked disheartened.

'You thought he would be here,' he said. 'Didn't you?'

'I thought he might,' I answered. 'But never mind. He could be lost in the woods. There's lots of places he could be. Maybe he's at home, waiting for you to come and feed him.'

He knew I didn't believe that, and I felt ashamed. It was wrong of me to raise his hopes. When we'd set out, I hadn't really expected to find the dog – I'd just wanted to give him something to do. Now I started on a systematic search, sending him off along side paths to check out ruined buildings and ditches; cutting away into the woods and leaving him to wander on his own; checking the boreholes at Bremner's, while he waited for me on the farm road. The boreholes were empty, dark and still in the mid-morning sunlight. I stopped for a moment. I liked it here: even in the clear light of day, there was something eerie about the place. Whenever I'd come out here as a child, I'd been aware of something: a flicker in the light, a ripple in the flow of time – the kind of thing children read about and believe without question, because the world has to be mysterious. I missed that, suddenly, and I wanted to be credulous again, to believe those folk stories and true-life accounts of local spirits and visitations they used to print in the Sunday papers.

When I got back to the farm road, Stewart was sitting under a tree with his head between his knees.

'Hey,' I called out. 'Are you asleep?'

He looked up.

'No,' he said. 'Did you find him?'

It looked like he'd been crying, and I felt awkward and guilty for having left him on his own. He was starting to give up – he'd probably known all along that Lassie was gone, but he hadn't been ready to accept the fact till now.

We crossed the next field and clambered over a barbed-wire fence that divided Bremner's farm from the scrubby heath beyond. It was a wild stretch of land, covered with low, twisted pines and patches of heather, and there were wide strips of burnt earth and vegetation where local kids had set fires, to watch them burn. We walked in silence. The sun was higher now and it was slow-going on the sandy tracks. I was glad when we came to the wide path that would take us back through the blueberry woods to the edge of town. All I wanted was to get Stewart home, and rescue the rest of the day.

I saw the shoes first. It seemed odd: a pair of brand-new tennis shoes set neatly on the path, as if someone had taken them off to go wading. Fifty yards further on, I saw a white T-shirt and a pair of navy-blue shorts. I looked around; there was nobody in sight. Stewart was walking behind me, with his head down – I don't think he even saw the clothes.

The body was some distance from the path, half-concealed

under a willow tree. I didn't know what it was at first, but I knew something was wrong. I got pretty close before I made him out: he was naked; his arms and legs were covered with bruises and when I got close I saw that his lips were swollen, as if he'd been punched in the mouth. He was about Stewart's age, maybe a little younger. His eyes looked remote, as if he was daydreaming, but I knew right away that he was dead. The odd thing was, I didn't feel shocked, or sick, or anything else people are supposed to feel when they find a body. I just felt sad and a little guilty, as if I were to blame, somehow, for what had happened to him.

I walked back to where Stewart was waiting for me. I didn't want him to see the dead boy.

'Listen,' I said, as briskly as I could, 'run down to Mr Bremner's and ask him to telephone the police. Ask him to get an ambulance too.'

Stewart didn't move.

'What is it?' He looked suspicious, as if he thought I was trying to divert him.

'It's all right,' I said. 'It's not Lassie. It's a kid. He's been hurt.'

He watched me. He was trying to decide if I was telling the truth. Then I saw the doubt in his eyes turn to fear – or not fear, but a kind of dismay.

'Is he dead?' he asked.

'No,' I answered, 'he's just hurt. Go on now. Run.'

He looked around. At first I thought he was scared to go on his own, then I realised he wasn't sure of the way. I pointed towards the farm road, and he turned and ran, as if his life depended on it.

I went back and stood by the body. I wanted to keep him company for a while, so he wouldn't be alone out there. Until that moment, I'd had an idea of an afterlife, a vague suspicion that people were better for being dead, emptied of fear and desire, observing from a distance the world they had just left, detached now, bound to the weather, to sunlight and mist and summer dewfalls, in the wet glitter of infinity. I hadn't really believed in a heaven, but I'd imagined some subtle and mutable state, a gradual evaporation of the spirit: transmigration, rebirth, some form of alchemy. Now I wasn't so sure. The dead boy looked very small: his body had dwindled somehow, like the dead rabbits and pheasants I'd seen on the road – already there was nothing left but the faint outline of a physical blueprint. The dead were bodies, pure and simple. If a soul had ever existed here, it was nothing personal, and now it was gone.

I found out later that Lassie had wandered further than usual. He had gone into the hills where a farmer had shot him for chasing sheep. I didn't tell Stewart about it, and after that day, he didn't mention the dog again.

The boy on the heath wasn't local. Nobody knew who he was: the police made an appeal for information, but nobody came forward. The story was in all the local papers, and it said two boys had found him, but neither of us was mentioned by name. The police had some questions for me, but they left Stewart out of it. To this day, I don't know if they ever identified the boy. I don't even know if he's buried, or if he's still in a mortuary somewhere, frozen and nameless.

Mum bought Stewart a pup for his next birthday – a barley-coloured, smiley dog, part retriever, part something else. He called it Sandy. He never talked about what I'd found on the heath – he must have known, but he didn't let on. It seemed to me that something about him had changed, but when I mentioned it, nobody else appeared to have noticed. Mum said it was natural that he should be a bit subdued, after the shock he'd had. But I thought it was something else. It's nothing I can put my finger on exactly – however I tell it, even to myself, it sounds fanciful. Nevertheless, I notice it sometimes in things he does and says. That feeling he had for the runt of the litter is gone. He looks out for himself now, and I tell myself that's a good thing, but I can't help thinking it's all too deliberate, as if he were trying to protect himself from something that might be lurking in the sunlight – as if he were afraid that, an arm's length away from the world he knows, there is a darkness he will never understand.

THE WEDDING CEILIDH

Liam and Aine wanted a summer wedding, but the old man was ill in the spring, and he decided he would see his daughter married before he died. I suppose in the days that followed, he regretted his haste: when Aine came home, on the night of her wedding, and moved back into her old room, she hung up her gown in her mother's wardrobe, alongside the dead woman's dresses, and Tommy sat in the kitchen, drinking whiskey till four in the morning, while the rain lashed at the windows, and no word came from Liam, or from those who were out looking for him. Aine didn't go out for several weeks after the wedding, and it broke Tommy's heart to see her, sitting in the front room, staring into space, pretending she was reading a book, or watching television. At the club, he'd say Liam Moone was a bad lot, that he'd always known there was something funny about him, but he never said this in front of Aine. He knew she was grieving; besides, he had liked Liam, everybody knew that, and they knew he was just as bewildered by what had happened as anybody else.

Liam Moone was quiet and easy-going, and something of a mystery, in his way. He liked a drink, but I never saw him drunk, and all the time he was engaged to Aine, he never looked at another woman. I knew him as well as anyone, I suppose – which wasn't much. I knew old Tommy too, and that was how

I came to play at the wedding – the old man and Liam had agreed that it ought to be a traditional affair, good music and a spot of dancing to make it a day to remember. I used to play at the club on a Friday night – Friday Night is Irish Night, the posters would say, and what that meant was me on the fiddle, Mickey Doyle on whistle and pipes and Pat Lavin on guitars. Sometimes Pat did a bit of singing, and Kevin McReynolds played drums if he was free. I didn't usually do weddings, but Tommy said he wanted the authentic sound, and he wasn't going to settle for anyone else. The funny thing was, our sound was far from authentic – some old-fashioned Irish tunes, certainly, but as much country and western as anything else, mixed up with a bit of sixties, and some Van Morrison covers for the younger crowd. Still, I wasn't going to argue; I knew I could use the money. I rehearsed some of the old songs with Pat, and Mickey said he could get us a proper singer, a friend of his sister's from college, called Cathy O'Brien. It rained for days before the wedding. There was flooding at Fulbrook and that morning, when we got to the club, there were inch-deep puddles all over the car park.

We pulled up as close to the door as we could but we still got pretty damp as we unloaded the gear.

'What a day for a wedding,' Pat said.

I looked at the sky. There was no sign of it letting up.

'Never mind,' I replied. 'As long as Aine's happy.'

'As long as Tommy's happy, more like,' said Pat.

I'd seen Aine in town the day before. I'd always had a soft spot for her at school, but that afternoon she looked more beautiful than ever, and I experienced a twinge of jealousy when I met her, with one of her bridesmaids, her hair tied back with a pale-blue ribbon, her face damp with rain.

Mickey brought our new singer round while we were setting up. She was tall and slim, with curly dark hair and a light in her eyes, a gladness about her that was contagious. She'd dressed for the occasion – which was more than could be said for Mickey, in his sweatshirt and cords.

'Did you forget it was a wedding, Mick?' Pat asked him, but Mickey just smiled and shook his head.

It was raining even harder when the guests arrived, and there was a great coming and going with umbrellas to get them indoors without spoiling the dresses. Aine looked radiant and Liam was quite the new husband, smiling and shaking hands, and posing for pictures with the bridesmaids. We played for a while, then they all went through to the dining room for the food and the speeches, and I stepped out into the foyer for a quiet cigarette.

I've always enjoyed those moments, when I get away from the crowd and stand in a corridor or a car park somewhere, watching the rain or listening to the birds and the traffic. The foyer was narrow and dim: at one end, near the window, an array of notice boards was covered twice over with lists of football teams and announcements of charity events. Nobody ever bothered to take any of these down, they just pinned the new stuff over the top. I was standing there, idly reading a report on a recent sponsored walk, when I heard a voice behind me.

'Do you play requests, mister?'

I looked round to see who it was, but the woman who had spoken was nobody I recognised. She was small and thin and she had a contained look about her, the look animals sometimes have in zoos – the small cats, the hunters. Yet her eyes were bright, alive and shiny and compelling.

'That depends,' I said.

'On what?' There was a challenge in her voice, and I suspected she was slightly drunk.

'On who's asking,' I answered quietly.

'It doesn't matter who's asking,' she said, with a smile. 'All that matters is the song.'

'And what would the song be?' I asked.

'"She Moved Through the Fair."'

'I don't think I know you,' I said. 'Are you a friend of the bride's?'

She laughed.

'No,' she said. 'A friend of the groom's. An old friend.'

'Ah.' I studied her face. By now I was certain she was nobody I had ever met, and I was pretty sure she wasn't an invited guest at this wedding.

'Do you like weddings?' I asked her. I was trying to distract her from her request and, at the same time, I was intrigued by her, especially by her voice, and that light in her eyes.

'They're all right. Though I'm not sure about this one. My old man would always say he preferred a good funeral to a wedding. I mean – there's always the promise of tragedy when two people come together. Whereas, with a funeral, the tragedy's over and you can relax. At least that's what my old man used to say.'

She laughed softly.

'What do you think?' she asked.

I didn't say anything. We stood in silence for a moment, our presences drowned out by the sound and the darkness of the rain, then she glanced towards the dining room.

'Play the song,' she said. 'Get your girl to sing it.'

'I'm sorry,' I said, 'but I don't think it's appropriate.'

'Oh, it's appropriate,' she replied. 'It's entirely appropriate.'

She smiled again, then turned and walked to the door at the far end of the foyer, and stepped outside into the dark wet of the afternoon.

The guests emerged from the dining room in twos and threes,

wanting music and drink, crowding to the bar, or sitting at the tables around the edge of the room, talking and smoking and working up the energy for a dance. Liam and Aine were the first on to the floor, then the others followed, men cutting in and dancing with the bride, while Liam stood by, grinning, with his hands thrust into his trouser pockets. I'd almost forgotten the strange woman – she wasn't there in the hall, and I'd started to put it all down to a bad joke when, about an hour after the dancing started, the woman appeared in the doorway. Slowly, she worked her way across the room, finding gaps between the dancers, circling and shifting around, till she stood at the edge of the stage, looking up at me.

'You haven't played my song,' she called out, after we'd finished our number. By now, I was certain she was a gatecrasher, and I was just about to lean down and tell her she should go, when I caught sight of Liam, watching her. He was standing at the edge of the dance floor about ten yards away. A moment before, he'd been flushed and happy, pleased with himself, letting somebody else dance with the bride. Now, all of a sudden, his face was drained of colour and he was staring at the woman, his mouth half-open, as if he wanted to speak, or cry out to her across the noisy dance floor.

The woman saw me looking and turned. Then she laughed and spoke to me again.

'I'm a friend of Liam's,' she said. 'The song's for him. For old time's sake.'

The others were starting up behind me. In any other circumstances, I would have said something to humour her, to get her away from the stage, but from the look on Liam's face, and from something in her manner, I knew there would be a scene unless I did what she wanted.

'All right,' I said. 'What was it again?'

She smiled and shook her head.

'You know what it was,' she said.

I straightened up and turned to Cathy. She was standing with her head to one side, listening, as if she were miles away, but I was pretty sure she'd overheard the whole conversation.

'Can you sing "She Moved Through the Fair?"' I asked her.

'What, now?'

I nodded.

'It's a bit of a change of pace,' she said.

'It's a request,' I replied. 'A friend of the groom.'

'All right, then.' She glanced down at the crowd of dancers, gave me a look that was meant to say on your head be it, swung her hair back and stepped up to the mike.

'We're going to slow it down a little now, folks,' she said.

People had stopped dancing and were turned to the stage now, watching us curiously. I suppose they imagined there was a trick coming, or another speech from the bride's father. Some looked a little fazed when I played the intro, and Cathy closed her eyes and began singing, while Pat and Mickey put up their instruments.

I glanced across at Liam. He was standing away from the crowd now, his head bowed, so I couldn't see his face, but I knew he was listening. The others were listening too; after the initial surprise, they had fallen into the mood, and they seemed to appreciate the introduction of this melancholy note, a moment for thoughts and memories, and a sweet, fleeting sadness. Half of them were homesick for places they had never known, for fishing towns and dairy farms they had only seen in pictures, or glimpsed from a car on a two-week holiday to Kerry or Donegal. They knew home existed somewhere, but they weren't quite sure what it was. It was only a dream of belonging, but it was the best they had, and if Cathy gave them an illusion of kinship for a few minutes, they were happy to take what they could, and not think too hard about it. For the first time that day, I realised how fine her voice was. She struck just the right tone, haunting and mysterious, yet suitably distant, as if she belonged to another time, or to no time or place at all. It was as if nothing mattered in this world where we found ourselves: everything was a story, a fragment of dreaming. I looked around for the woman I'd met in the foyer, but she had gone and, when I turned to where Liam had been standing, I saw that he too had vanished. I looked for Aine. She was standing by her father, holding his arm, swaying to the music. She seemed not to have noticed her new husband's disappearance, and I only hoped that Liam would get rid of his woman and come back, before anyone else figured out what was going on.

The old stories have endings, even when they're mysterious or frightening. That's how it is in the old country, things always happen a generation away and the people of that time are always capable of improbable shifts and transformations. When the strange girl comes to the farmer's bed, just as she promised, the neighbours hear his cry for miles in the snowy dusk, and that night, over the fields, they see wandering fires, pale and wet and subtle in the moonlight, as the fox people come to the chosen house for their yearly feast. Or perhaps a man comes up from the sea, and lives in their midst all winter: wherever he goes, there's a shadow beside him, the colour of something hard and misshapen that has lain years underwater; his eyes are bright and green, some people say his fingers are webbed or his skin is smooth and silvery, like fish-scales. He bides his time till Candlemas, then he leaves and one of the village girls follows him into the fog. Her sand-filled dress is discovered

165

at daybreak, between the lines of fishnets and the sea, or an old man finds her, crouched in the lee of his upturned boat; she is wild-eyed, speechless, old before her time. Nine months later a child is born, and it lies silent in its crib, unwanted, gazing through a veil of eelskin. In the old country, our sins and errors are turned into stories of transformation. There's no room for judgment.

The old stories have endings, but our lives aren't like that – they're messy and inconclusive, and sometimes people disappear for no reason. I wish I could say for sure what happened to Liam. I heard rumours – that he'd been hurt in a disturbance at a squat, that he'd cut someone in a fight outside a bar. I heard that two other men and a woman were involved, but nobody knew the details. I only heard these things months after the wedding and, as far as I knew, Aine was unaware of what was going on. When Tommy died, she inherited the house and quite a bit of money – a lot more than anyone had expected. She didn't get a divorce; she didn't go out with other men; she stayed at home, and it seemed to me she was waiting for him to return, even though she knew he never would. I used to go round and see her some-times, and she'd welcome me in, give me a cup of tea, and listen to my stories about the band, and how well we were doing. She never once mentioned Liam. I think she managed to convince herself, at least some of the time, that he'd disappeared into one of those old stories and, if he had, then an ending would come, sooner or later. I think she imagined him travelling in the dark, caught up in some strange magic that nobody could have resisted, or even explained. He wanted to come home, he just didn't know how. Maybe what really happened was even a little like that: seen from a distance, it would be ugly, but close-up, in his own mind, it probably felt like something else, like part of a story that could only be told in a lie, or a fairy tale, or the words of an old-time song.

DADA

When he was still alive, I would never have imagined that I'd end up keeping Dada. He had this smell about him that I didn't like, a surface layer of soap and hair cream that didn't quite hide the damp animal scent underneath. I still remember sitting at the table while he sucked food into his mouth, gulping and slobbering, only pausing to gasp for breath between mouthfuls. Then, after dinner, he would sit in the big chair and watch television. Sometimes I'd get interested in a programme, and he would reach for the remote and switch channels. He liked quizzes and game shows best: he'd sit muttering to himself, with a glass of whisky in his hand, trying to guess the answers to the questions. Sometimes he'd repeat what the contestants said, pretending he'd thought of it first; or he'd make little gasping sounds, little oohs and ahs, as if the answer was on the tip of his tongue. He'd look up at the row of books on the window sill – books he'd probably never even opened – as if he could extract the answers from them by a kind of osmosis. The books didn't belong to him. They were the property of the dead: two bibles, a picture dictionary, an almanac, a copy of Mrs Beeton. They'd been on that window sill for years and they were thick with dust and condensation, decaying where they stood, propped up between two chunks of limestone.

Before they died, I had Granny and Bella for my friends.

Now only Dada's left, I've laid him out nicely in the downstairs bathroom, so he won't have to go to the graveyard. I put ice in the bath to keep him cold; I make it in the freezer, in those big Tupperware boxes Granny used to have for keeping cakes fresh, and there's some novelty plastic elephants, filled with quick-freezing liquid, that I put around his face. Sometimes I make myself a cup of coffee and I go and sit with him for a while, in the middle of the day. Occasionally I read to him from the papers, but mostly I just talk. It always helps to talk about your troubles, and sometimes it feels like a real conversation. It's certainly more of a conversation than any we ever had when he was alive. I used to ask him the same questions I ask now: I wanted to know if Karen was my mother, and who Granny was, and why I called him Dada, if he wasn't my father. But he wouldn't tell me anything. Even when he was drunk, he'd just talk rubbish about religion and politics, and stuff he'd seen on television. Sometimes he laughed at me; he'd say the truth was staring me in the face, only I couldn't see it. He said the truth is always there, just staring us in the face. I ask him about that sometimes, and I look at his mouth, as if he could answer. I know he's dead; I know he can't speak; but then, nobody really knows what 'dead' means – you hear about people in comas, how they're there, just below the surface, and who's to say death isn't like that? He can't talk to me, but maybe now, at last, he can hear what I'm saying: maybe, just by listening, he's giving me the chance to figure things out for myself.

Bella was Granny's sister. She died when I was nine, but I still remember her. She was tall and very thin, and she still had gold in her hair. She liked looking after the garden: she had this collection of auriculas that she grew in a long row along the edge of the path. She was the only one who was ever kind to us when I lived with Karen. I stayed there for six years and, in all that time, Bella was our only visitor. I think she loved Karen, in spite of everything that happened. She used to bring us presents, things that had belonged to her for years, that she said she didn't want any more: pieces of glass and polished stone, paperweights, mirrors – anything that caught and reflected the light. Sometimes she'd take me to the pictures. Whenever there was trouble, she'd come and stay at our house, and she would sit up all night with Karen, talking to her quietly, trying to get her to explain what was wrong.

I don't like to think about Karen. At one time, I thought *she* was my mother. I knew something was wrong with her: she used to give me her pills and tell me they were sweets, so I'd eat them and get sick; once, she made a cut in her arm and sat in the front room watching the blood come out. When I wet the bed, she made me kneel on the floor in my wet pyjamas, or she wrapped the wet sheet around my shoulders and made me sit in the bottom of the airing cupboard. When I was five, she took me to Edinburgh and left me on Princes Street. One minute she was there, then all of a sudden she was gone. I was glad when they told me she wasn't my real mother, and I came here to live with Granny. Dada didn't want me but, as long as Bella and Granny were around, he couldn't do anything about it.

My best memory of that time is of helping Bella in the garden. I was frightened of the garden at first. I always thought somebody else was out there, watching us: I'd keep turning round to the lilac tree by the fence, but all I ever saw was Dada coming in from the field, wiping his hands on an old handkerchief. I was frightened of him too. He never spoke, he would just stare at me, as if I was some stray animal the women had taken in. I sometimes thought, if Bella hadn't been there, he would have killed me with his spade, the way I once saw him kill a rat he caught, in the corner of the yard.

★　　★　　★

In the afternoons, when Dada is sleeping, I watch old films on television. It reminds me of the matinees we used to go to, in the old picture house in town. Sometimes I close my eyes at the beginning of the film, and I'm back at the Odeon, sitting next to Bella in the cheap seats, smelling her, all womanly, with her perfume and hair-lacquer smell. The usherette would come round with a torch, shining it across the rows, under the silvery-blue light from the projection room. I loved when it shone on us, and it felt like we were being seen, like the people in the film, and I loved how everything was so sweet and warm, like being in a room made of sugar.

I didn't go to the pictures after Bella died. Instead, I would sit in the kitchen, with my eyes closed, listening to the films on television. I'd wait a long time – sometimes I'd wait till the film was almost finished – then I'd open my eyes: I always knew when to look, there would be something in the soundtrack that pulled me in, so I'd slip past the reality of Dada's house and into the picture. A shot, a cry, the sound of laughter – something would pull me into the life of the killer or the hero, and I'd watch for a while before I closed my eyes again, sealing a moment of the story in the clear black and white of my mind. If the film was in colour, I'd keep my eyes shut all the way through, just listening to the voices and imagining them in black and white. Colour was too difficult. When I tried thinking in colour I'd remember Karen and get upset. Or I'd think of Dada, asleep upstairs, and I'd feel sick.

Dada. That's what they taught me to call him, and that's what I've had to call him all my life, a grown person trapped in the language of a child. Once, when I called him Grandfather, he got really angry and stamped out of the house. He sulked for days afterwards; he started doing everything for himself, making

174

his own lunch, spilling food on the floor and leaving it to rot or get trodden in, letting on he didn't need me to look after him. He wanted me to know that he wouldn't be trapped into answering questions – and he was right, I'd only called him Grandfather to see how he'd react. You get that closed in with somebody, they can read your thoughts. It's not as if he was completely stupid. In his way, he was interested in knowledge – the problem was, he didn't know what information he had, or what to do with it. Whenever we got some new gadget for the kitchen, he would try to learn the instructions in all the different languages on the leaflet, but he'd always get it wrong, so he almost knew the Danish for *Do not boil in this container*, or the Italian for *This product is dishwasher-proof*. He used to buy boxes of Swiss chocolates and memorise the words for pistachio or cherry cream in German and French. Sometimes he got things mixed up. He'd make ridiculous statements, and I never bothered to disagree with him, because of how nasty he could be. If we had an argument, he'd say it was his house and if I didn't like it there, I could go find somewhere else to live. A couple of times I went upstairs and started to pack, but then I looked round and saw all Bella's things and I knew I had to stay, because they looked so nice the way I kept them and I knew he wouldn't look after them properly. Some of it was good stuff, too: a pair of little Chinese bowls with fishes inside, a clock on the hall table, where you could see the works, shiny brass cogs and wheels under a glass dome.

He was at his worst when he drank. He'd walk down to the pub every day; when he got home he'd be so drunk he'd fall down, and I'd have to get out of bed to make sure he wasn't hurt. A couple of times he was sick on the kitchen floor; one night he fell downstairs and I ran out to see if he was all right, but he just stood up again and went out to the kitchen for a drink. When he made a mess, he wouldn't clean it up. I'd go down some mornings and find milk and broken glass all over the floor, or I'd find little puddles in the bathroom where he'd missed the toilet. Once I found a hard little turd on the landing – just the one, neat and dry, like poodle dirt.

Granny didn't die of natural causes. You could say she was murdered, really; she wasn't killed right away but her injuries were extensive: fractured skull, severe bruising to the face and chest, glass in one eye, severed ear, ruptured spleen, damage to the lungs, both legs broken. She'd been involved in a collision on Westfield Bridge; the police told us the other driver was speeding, so it was his fault, but I overheard someone telling his wife he'd died instantly, and wouldn't have suffered any pain. I saw his picture, afterwards, in the local paper: he was quite a nice-looking man, with a smiley face and wet, puppy-dog eyes. I cut the article out and put it away in the chest of drawers: sometimes, when Dada was at the pub, I'd take it out and look at the deceased, trying to find some ill-intent, some hint of madness.

Granny took longer to die, so she didn't get her picture in the papers. I remember clearly the one time I saw her conscious. She was lying in intensive care, surrounded by bags and tubes, and those wavy machines, like the ones you see on television. It was just me at the time; suddenly, she opened her eyes and looked up, and I think she knew what was happening to her, I could see she was on the verge of panic, like an actress who's forgotten her lines, or even what the play is about. A moment later, Dada came in: when she saw him, Granny closed her eyes, and the life just flowed out of her, as if a switch had been thrown in her mind. That was all Dada needed. The look on his face when he went to fetch the nurse, the way he moved, the way he spoke: everything betrayed his hope that this tragedy would finally give him what he'd wanted all along – a position, a stance, a way of being in the world. He loved the way the nurses treated him – all that sympathy. After she died, he perfected his act over a period of months: dignified, unashamed, as wounded now as he'd always pretended to be. Maybe that's a bit hard; I could see he was frightened too, and perhaps he was hurt, after his fashion; yet I could also see he was grateful that something had happened to him, even if he wasn't quite sure how convincing it was.

We lived like that for a while, just the two of us, locked into the dead house together. He'd drink away the money and I'd keep house and watch television. Maybe nothing would have changed if Corinne hadn't started coming round. She lived about half a mile along the main road, in one of the farm cottages that used to belong to the estate. She was a strange-looking girl, but I liked her: she was funny and she'd come and talk to me sometimes when Dada wasn't there. She was only a kid – about twelve, I suppose – but she'd have make-up on: lipstick, black mascara, that kind of thing, and she'd wear these thin silky dresses and high-heeled shoes that she borrowed from her mother. The make-up was pretty good; it looked like she'd been done by a professional. Sometimes she had black lines around her eyes, like Elizabeth Taylor in *Cleopatra*. Her hair was thick and curly, and black as coal, and she'd brush it out so it stood on end, like it was full of static. Everything about her was exaggerated: her eyes were huge; she had this amazing sexy mouth, like a young Hedy Lamarr; her skin was smooth as soap. Sometimes she'd wear a plain white dress, like a shroud, and she'd lie on the wall in the yard, pretending to be dead. It was amazing how she'd change then, her skin was so white it reflected everything: you could see the green of the hedge on her cheeks and forehead. She really looked beautiful.

I tried to keep our friendship a secret. I didn't want Dada knowing about her; I knew he would do something to spoil it. We were happy in our own little world. We'd go into the outhouse or the barn and look for rats to kill; if we didn't find any, we'd catch lacewings and flies, but never spiders, because Corinne didn't think we should kill spiders. I liked catching lacewings: most of the time they'd come to rest in high corners, they were pale and insubstantial, like ghosts. Corinne said they were the forms the dead took when they were travelling between one life and another.

Corinne says time is going to end soon. She says it's just about to reach the point when it's all right to stop – it's like a magic trick, it's not really happening, and any minute now things will change, like when the magician pulls back the curtains or opens the magic box, and the rabbit or his beautiful assistant has vanished. Everything will collapse into that moment. It will be some ordinary event that finally causes time to stop: you might be walking home late some afternoon, just as the streetlamps are coming on, when a stranger in a top hat and tails – an ugly, middle-aged man with damp, paper-white hands hidden under his white kid gloves – a complete stranger with a winning smile steps out of the shadows and offers you a cigarette. You take it; he reaches into his pocket and pulls out a box of matches – and everything ends. She says it's not like dying, it's more like the moment after you die, when you suddenly become indifferent to everything that ever mattered to you. The magician strikes a match and lights your cigarette with a soft, conspiratorial smile. It's too late to go back, or change your mind: time has stopped, and you relax, you shrug off a feeling that's been with you for years, a vague anxiety that you could never quite shake before: though now the end has come, you realise it could have happened any time.

I told Corinne about Dada, how she should watch out for him and not come round when he was there. Things went pretty well until one afternoon when he came home early from the pub and caught us mucking around in the downstairs bathroom. It was raining outside, so I had invited her in. I think Dada got the wrong idea, because we'd taken our clothes off so they wouldn't get wet, and he got angry and hit me. Then he went into the kitchen and just sat there crying and saying he didn't know what he was going to do with me, how he was going to have to put me in an institution. As usual he was drunk. Corinne got dressed and went home, and I went upstairs to Bella's room. I was used to him talking like that, it didn't bother me, but I was ashamed of him in front of Corinne, and I decided to teach him a lesson. I kept thinking how it would have been if I'd had a real father, like other people: the kind of father who would take me swimming or fishing; the kind of father I could trust, like the fathers in movies who knew how to look after horses or climb mountains. At seven o'clock I heard him moving around, getting ready to go out. I went downstairs and took the house key out of his pocket, then I asked him what he wanted for dinner, but he didn't answer, he just put on his jacket and started for the door. 'Feed the birds,' was all he said. Then he went out to spend our money at the pub.

After he'd gone, I went out into the yard and looked at the pigeons for a long time. Corinne said you shouldn't keep birds in a cage, no matter how big it was – they'd be better off dead, she said. The funny thing was, though they were Dada's pigeons, and he was supposed to be so proud of them and everything, it was always my job to feed them. Sometimes he'd bring one of

his cronies back from the pub and show the birds off, as if he
was the one who looked after them, but he never mentioned
the work I did.

The rain had stopped by then, but the grass was wet and
runnels of water streamed off the roof of the outhouse, and
I could hear the pigeons, cooing and fluttering around. They
seemed restless. In the end, I couldn't take it any more, them
being caged up in there, and I opened the door, so they could
fly free if they wanted. For a while, they just fluttered around
in the cage, or sat on their perches, as if they hadn't noticed
anything different. One or two got out, and I watched them
wheeling above the roof, looking confused, as if they didn't
know which way to go. I wanted them to fly away, to vanish
into the distance, towards the sea, or the open sky, but most
of them just stayed where they were, and I went back indoors
in disgust.

I sat in the big chair, in the dark kitchen, waiting. It was a
wet night: from time to time, an owl called across the yard,
and once I heard a vixen on the hill, crying like a banshee
for her mate. Dada got home around one o'clock. I heard
him stumbling about in the yard, then I heard his hand on
the door, leaning to steady himself while he went through
his pockets, looking for his key. I stood on the other side
of the door: I could hear him breathing, just inches away,
and I wondered if he could hear me. I held my breath. He
began muttering to himself, but I couldn't understand what he
was saying, it was like some foreign language, or somebody
talking in tongues. It was quite funny really, looking back.
Because he was sulking, he didn't want to shout for me to
come and open the door, so he just kept on rummaging
through his pockets, talking to himself and getting wet. It

was ages before he remembered about the spare key in the outhouse and staggered back across the yard, banging up against everything he'd knocked into on the way in. I moved over to the window and looked out. He pushed open the outhouse door and stumbled inside.

I unlocked the door quickly and ran across the yard. Dada had fallen over; he was on his hands and knees, trying to get up, mumbling, soaked to the skin. I don't think he even knew I was there. I pulled the door shut, snapped the padlock on the latch, and ran back out of the rain. Then I put the kettle on and made myself a cup of tea. It was that good tea he didn't like, from the delicatessen.

Later, the wind picked up and howled around the house – it made me think of that old film about Scott of the Antarctic: John Mills leading his doomed expedition into the blizzard; Captain Oates getting up and stepping outside for a moment. I started my search in Dada's bedroom: it was just as Granny had left it, with its smell of toilet water and brass, and the Sacred Heart on the wall, above the chest of drawers. I thought I would discover something there, some secret document, a birth certificate, a marriage licence, a pile of old letters or photographs, but all I found were Granny's old skirts and blouses, and Dada's clothes, all musty with smoke and grime: shirts and trousers, underwear and shoes, lying in a heap at the bottom of his wardrobe, and several pairs of old-fashioned paisley pyjamas, still in their cellophane wrappers from years ago. There was other stuff, too, that I had never seen him wear: a good suit, a row of silk ties, a cummerbund, a pair of swimming trunks. It was an odd feeling, going through those things: it was like finding a ghost in the house, or discovering that somebody else had been there all along, without my knowing.

★   ★   ★

In the morning, I went down to see how he was. I thought he would be sorry for what he'd done, and I'd forgive him and make him breakfast. I went round the back to see how many of the pigeons had flown away – the cage was empty, but there was a dead bird on the floor and a mess of feathers in one corner, so I reckoned something had got in there during the night and scared them off. I was sorry for that. I didn't know how Dada would take it.

As soon as I opened the outhouse door, I knew something was wrong. For one thing, he was half-sitting, half-lying on the floor, and he looked odd, as if he wasn't really a person at all, just a dummy that somebody had left there, propped against the wall. He'd slumped to one side, and his face was very white, with black around his mouth and eyes. I didn't believe it at first – I thought it was some kind of trick – but eventually I realised he was dead. I kicked his leg a couple of times, then I bent down and put my ear next to his mouth to see if he was breathing. He smelled of beer and onions. I touched his face. He hadn't bothered to shave before he went out, and it felt funny, that cold stubble. Stupid bastard, I said. I thought it was his fault that he'd died – I still do, really. I know it was me who locked him out, but I didn't see that he had any reason to die. Maybe he did it to spite me.

That was when the idea came to me, to bring him in and keep him in the bathroom, so nobody would know what had happened. I suppose I was frightened – I thought if anybody saw him, they'd think it was my fault – but there was more to it than that. I was sure, if I looked after him, he wouldn't have to be completely dead. He wouldn't be able to go to the pub any more, but he would still be at home, and I'd treat him well, I'd read him the paper and tell him about the films I'd seen on television. I thought I'd put him in the downstairs bathroom, because that was the coldest place in the house, and he'd be all right in the bath. Maybe, when he was more settled, I could show Corinne.

Some people would think it odd, keeping him like this, but I don't see why. It isn't fair, that we have to give up our dead so quickly: it's good to keep them around for a while, for a long time even, to get to know them better. That way, we can decide what to do for the best: Bella would have been happier if we'd put her out in the garden, to feed her auriculas, and I think Dada's better off in the bath than he would be in the graveyard. I look after him. If I've been out for the day, I go in to see him as soon as I get back. I brush off the craneflies and dust, and start from where I left off, talking to him, washing his skin, replacing the ice around his body. It's a long process, but I'm determined to make someone new, and now that he is in my mind, I can see him differently. I can trace him back to an origin I must have forgotten was there: a bright afternoon, a beach, Dada in his dark-red swimming trunks, taking me into the water and telling me I needn't be frightened because he's with me, he'll hold me up – and he does, he puts his hands under my body, and all of a sudden I can swim, just by doing what he says. When he takes his hands away I feel this amazing lightness, I am weightless and free, and surprised at myself, because this freedom comes from an unexpected abandonment, from letting his hands support me, then letting the water take over where he leaves off. He seems, at this moment, to be so knowing, so generous, but then, so am I – I am the one who's traced him back to that origin, then carried him forward on a different path from the one he took. I'm making him the gift of a new life: I'm teaching him to be something he never even dreamed of becoming. Some time soon, I'll show him to

Corinne, and I'll tell her what kind of man he really was, how he taught me things and took me swimming. Then I'll bathe him one last time and leave him there, so his soul can move on to something new.

BEBOP

The summer I turned thirteen, I'd go round to Bill McCabe's house and listen to jazz on Saturday mornings. It started with him giving me little jobs to do around the place – washing his car, setting traps for mice, weeding his wife's rose beds – but that was only a pretext. He'd call me over once or twice a month, and when I'd finished my chores, he'd take me into the front room and play me a record. He'd give me money for the work I did, but the music was my real payment. Every time I went there, he played something different. He had a wide range of stuff, but he liked bebop more than anything, and he'd talk about Charlie Parker the way the teachers in school talked about Jesus. A few of the tasks he gave me to do were pretty pointless. I think he just wanted someone to talk to about jazz, because his wife hated it, and nobody else in that town had even heard of Dizzy Gillespie. Sometimes he told me things, stuff he knew about from his job at Connell's. He'd show me how mercury worked, rolling it round in a saucer, trying to get me to believe it was metal. Or he showed me how to nip the head off a flower and suck out the nectar, a thin sweetness that stayed in my throat for hours, like the taste of the host at Mass. He'd share these moments of insight, these small revelations, as if they were hugely important, then we'd stand there in awkward silence, wondering what to say next. I didn't know how lonely he was till it was too late.

He once said I took too much for granted, but it didn't matter, because that was the particular gift of the thirteen-year-old, to take things for granted while he still could. Those were the actual words he used. At the time, I didn't understand much of what he said. What mattered was the music. If I'm grateful for anything, it's for those afternoons, sitting in Bill McCabe's front room, not saying anything, listening to John Coltrane play 'Summertime'.

It was The Feather Lady who found Patsy Allan one August morning, out by Fulbrook Pond. We called her The Feather Lady because we didn't know what else to call her. Nobody knew her real name, so we identified her by the battered old hat she wore wherever she went: a man's felt hat from the look of it, made ladylike by the addition of several peacock feathers tucked into the band. She had gone out to the pond around dawn, as she often did, dressed in her finery, with her nets and baskets, her coat pockets crammed with stale bread and apple cores. At first, she had missed the body, though it must have been in plain view; she was busy, she said, listening for the fishes, scenting the water to see what kind of day it was going to be. It must have cost her something to report what she found. She was one of those women you saw in towns like ours, shy and secretive, cautious of strangers, destined all their lives for a long middle age of cats and books on sugarcraft. Usually she did all she could to keep the world at a distance, to make it seem she was just a visitor, a short-term guest, just passing through and not likely to get in anybody's way. But when she saw the girl, she knew she had to do something, and she ran along the road to the bakery and called for Mr Gaston, who telephoned the police, then walked back to the pond with her, to see the thing for himself.

The body was exactly where she'd said it was, on the far side of the pond, half-concealed by the overhanging branches of a willow. Whoever had put it there could hardly have believed the police would consider it a simple case of drowning – not with the bruises on Patsy's face and thighs, the tears in her clothes, the red lines on her wrists where it looked like someone had bound her. Half the town had been searching for Patsy for two days, ever since she'd failed to arrive home from her friend Marianne's fifteenth birthday party. Different people had gone by the pond at different times, and there had been no sign of a body then, so whoever it was, he must have killed her somewhere else, then carried her to the pond and left her face-down in the water, in her pink and white party dress. He could easily have done this at night. He could have driven up with the girl in the boot of his car and dropped her into the pond when no one was watching. That was the closest I could get to forming an image of the killer: a man in a dark coat, standing beside his car, smoking a cigarette, like the killer in a film. He would have waited till the coast was clear before he carried Patsy to the pond and pushed her in. Then he would have driven away calmly, while the ripples were still spreading over the water.

The adults wouldn't talk about it when children were around. I remember how odd it was, pretending nothing had changed. I'd hardly known Patsy – she was a couple of years older than me – but all of a sudden I had memories of her, of seeing her in Brewster's, of the slight singsong in her voice. One afternoon, in the maths class, I suddenly became convinced that the book I was using had once been hers. I looked at the inside cover, but there was only one name there besides mine, a boy's name, and no other marks except for a faded doodle, a five-pointed star drawn in blue-black ink, formal and precise, like a symbol in alchemy.

The adults didn't talk about it, but at the same time, there was an air of expectancy in the town, as if people were waiting for Patsy to come walking back along the High Street in her party dress, afraid she would be punished for having stayed away so long. Just as the police were piecing together the last hours of her life, so we were recreating her from wisps of memory, perhaps from guilt that no one had seen her go, or from a refusal to accept what had happened. It was a forensic process, a reconstruction, a whole community attempting the willed resurrection of someone most of us barely knew.

I never found out how The Strip got its name, or why anybody had even bothered to give it a separate name of its own at all. It was only a piece of land, a huddle of poor houses and overgrown allotments at the end of a long dusty road that ran on for a few miles and disappeared into a turnip field. Officially it was still part of Weldon; at another, subtler level, it had its own special character. It was like a village in a horror film: the windows looked empty; all you could see was rusty machinery and waist-high grass where there should have been lawns; abandoned toys lay in the road, like the evidence from some Sunday-tabloid crime. It was easy to imagine a maniac in every house, to catch glimpses of the sinister, inbred kin in their bare kitchens, talking about poisons and traps, surrounded by damp, half-naked children and ugly, malevolent dogs. When Mr Brewster asked if I wanted a paper round, I jumped at the chance of some extra money. He waited till I'd agreed before he told me where it was, and by then it was too late. I'd heard stories about The Strip – the baby in the dustbin, the woman locked in the burning house – but they sounded pretty unlikely, and besides, I'd already spent the money, in my mind.

The first morning was pretty difficult. There was one street

I couldn't find, and when I stopped a man to ask for directions, he only snarled and kept on walking. There were some nasty-looking dogs, too; but the worst thing that happened was when an old woman came to her door and tried to get me to go inside. She looked a bit crazy: there was a dribble of blood on her dress and I could smell the incontinence from where I was standing. I told her I was busy, I had to deliver the papers, and she started to cry, waving her arms about wildly, as if they were wings and she was trying to get them to work. She started calling me Tommy. I remember the way she looked at me, angry and desperate and confused all at once – she kept telling me to go in, trying to find some bond, some obscure complicity she must have believed existed between us.

After they found Patsy, my mother wanted me to give up the round. I had to go out when it was still quite dark, and I suppose she was afraid the killer would strike again. The Chief Constable had been on the radio, warning everyone to be vigilant, especially young women. It was difficult convincing my mother I wasn't in any danger. As far as I was concerned, the killer would be long gone and, anyway, The Strip wasn't as bad as everybody made out.

'I wasn't thinking about *that*,' she said. 'I'm more worried about the cars, at that time of the morning.'

I smiled. For my mother, everything that happened was an accident that could be prevented if you didn't tempt fate by talking about it. If you took precautions, they had to be for something unlikely, never for the possible. Whenever anything bad happened to someone, she would find some outlandish explanation for why it affected that person, and not somebody else. I overheard her telling my cousin Madeleine that Patsy had been seen with a cigarette in her hand the night she died. For her, that explained everything. She really believed any evil

191

could be avoided, if you took the most absurd measures: she had a cupboard in the kitchen that was full of old medicines – kaolin and morphine, witch hazel, flowers of sulphur, Dettol, California Syrup of Figs, bottles whose labels had been lost, crusted at the rim with thick, creamy sediments. For as long as I could remember, this hoard had been there, unused and out of reach, but magical, like a talisman, protecting us against every imaginable horror, except the mild discomforts they were originally intended to allay.

Every Saturday, cousin Madeleine would come to visit and I would flee to the garden or Bill McCabe's house. It made me feel special, sitting in his front room by the big old radiogram, listening to Lester Young. I would dream about foreign cities, the smell of the American night, and dark cars parked on empty roads, like in the films. When I listened to bebop, I had a sense of the distance, a remoteness from other people like that dreamy feeling when I'd hardly slept all night; how my skin would feel chalky and warm, and the wind would be cool on my face when I stood at the window. This music was all air and distance and infinite possibility. Looking back, I understand that I didn't really know Bill, I confused him with his record collection. I was impressed by how much he knew about jazz, and the fact that he didn't talk much. Mrs McCabe would bring me a cup of coffee and a plate of biscuits, then she'd go back to the kitchen or the garden and leave us to it. If I tried to make conversation while the music was playing, Bill just gave me a polite look, smiled, then went back to listening. I know now he was passing on the one thing he valued. I also suspect it wasn't really personal: if it hadn't been me, it would have been someone else. The only thing that mattered was the fact that I liked jazz.

I think I knew at the time that they couldn't have children.

It didn't seem to bother them, they were far too busy with what they were doing, and I couldn't see that it mattered. Bill was tall and heavy; he drank coffee all the time; you could never tell what was going on in his mind. When he sat down, he gave himself up entirely to gravity. I felt safe in his house. It was a tidy, comfortable space for people to live in; nobody made a fuss if I spilled coffee or made crumbs. After a while, I started to take it for granted.

We weren't supposed to talk about Patsy, but we still gathered at the pond in the afternoons to look at the place where the body was found. We'd go in twos and threes – never alone – and stand by the water, talking quietly: conspirators; detectives. Everyone said they'd know the killer on sight: what he would look like, how he would sound if he walked into Brewster's and asked for a newspaper or a packet of cigarettes. There would be something that gave him away, a softness about his hands, a shadow in his eyes, a fleck of spit at the corner of his mouth. We hung around the pond because we knew from the cinema that the murderer always revisits the scene of his crime; we stood outside Brewster's in the evening because the man would want to buy a paper every day, to see if the police were on to him. Meanwhile, though we never admitted it, what we really wanted was a chance to see the ghost or, worse still, a repetition, someone we knew, someone our age, gazing up through the water with a scarf around her neck, serene and distant, like the corpses in films. The police made statements from time to time, but as the days passed, we decided they would never catch the murderer.

We each had our own ideas about who had killed Patsy: someone from The Strip; a gypsy; a man from another town; a sex pervert. We had always known there were strangers who passed through our world: they were the ones who lit fires in the woods, the ones who hung rats and crows in the hedges, marking the borders no child should cross. When I wandered too far from home, I knew to turn back when I found those signs. Those people were always gone when I arrived, the only evidence of their passing would be a box of matches or a lacing of fire in the grass. Sometimes they stayed in one place for days at a time. Once I walked out to the derelict church on the other side of the railway line: it had been boarded up for years, but that day I could see someone had been there – the grass was littered with spent cartridges, torn clothes, rain-sloshed photographs ripped from magazines. There was an old sign on the door to say all the valuables had been removed, but the boards on one window had been pulled away, and I could see into the damp, stripped interior. There were delicate heads carved into the stone above the arches and dark veins on the wall where the ivy had been pulled away. In the windows, the jagged remnants of stained glass glittered in the sunlight. The church had been deconsecrated, then taken over by phantoms. It was like entering a forbidden room, just climbing up into the window and looking in; I was a little scared and impressed with myself, when I dropped through and stood in the dark interior, tracing a bright trail of new blood and spent matches to a bundle of old clothes and new magazines in the space behind the altar.

The next victim was a girl from The Strip. Her name was Cathy Reynolds: she was a small, plump girl, not very pretty, just out of school. She had started work at the bakery just two weeks before she disappeared. I'd seen her a couple of times on my round, but she didn't speak. I said hello and she looked straight through me. I don't think she was very bright. I was a bit surprised that the killer chose her, to be honest: after all, he could have gone after any girl he wanted.

They found the body in a ditch about two miles from her

house, but she hadn't been killed there. The police said she might have accepted a lift from her attacker, and the man had taken her somewhere and dumped the body several hours later. There were rumours that she'd been tortured: she had cuts and burns on her arms and chest, and some of her fingernails had been pulled out. Two boys from our school found the body and they had seen everything – the cuts, the burns, the bruises on her legs. They told everybody that Cathy was naked.

I saw Mrs Reynolds a few days later. She was sitting in her front room with the light on and the curtains open at six o'clock in the morning: she looked like she'd been there all night. I was delivering across the street and I could see her plain: small and fat, in a pale blue dressing gown, she looked like an older version of Cathy, sitting on the sofa, gazing out at the morning rain. I don't know if she saw me; if she did, she gave no sign. She had a box of matches in her hand: as I looked up, she struck one and let it burn, without looking at it, then she shook it out, let it fall, and struck another. She must have struck eight or ten matches while I stood watching. Every time she lit one I saw her face: she was ghostly white, it looked as if the skin around her eyes had been dusted with flour or chalk, and I knew something was wrong – she wasn't just mourning, or whatever, she was really ill. The room was bare: no plants, no pictures on the walls, almost no furniture except the sofa and a low coffee table. I moved closer. I really felt sorry for her.

It was a while before she noticed I was there and even when she did, she didn't move, she just looked out at me, almost curiously, as if she was wondering whether I was the one who had killed her daughter, and for a moment, I felt quite guilty, as if I'd known what would happen all along, and done nothing to prevent it.

★   ★   ★

That night I had the first bad dream. I couldn't remember much when I woke up: I'd been crawling across the floor of the ruined church, grubbing around for candle stubs, finding spoor and the quicklimed flesh of the killer's other victims. I knew in the dream there were hundreds of bodies there, and I was crawling through their remains, tangles of bloody hair, torn clothes, fingernails, naked arms and legs. Next thing I knew I was sitting at the table in our kitchen at home. I could see clearly: it had been raining, but now the sun was out and the light was strong. A girl was standing by the door, as if she had just come in; she was wearing a long coat and blue gloves, but I could see on her neck, above the collar, a white flap of skin had peeled away, and I knew her whole body was like that under the coat. Only her face was unaffected. She was looking at me: it was as if she had just asked a question that I hadn't heard, and now she was waiting for my answer.

Without taking her eyes off me, she walked over to the table and sat down. I noticed it was bare, except for a salt cellar lying on its side, and a single fork. She took off one glove and held out her hand. It was white and the skin was flaking. I thought she was going to touch me, but she stayed where she was, reaching out one hand, as if she wanted me to touch her soft, flaking skin, and I almost wanted to do just that, to take her hand and feel the sores, in a moment of unexpected curiosity and love. But I stayed where I was and, for a moment, we remained suspended, like people in a photograph, frozen in a fault of time.

The next day I walked out along the road to the place where Cathy's body had been found. I didn't know what to expect, or even where to look, but it didn't take a detective to find the place. Somebody had been out there before me, having a picnic. I found some greaseproof paper, a slice of tomato, a curl of orange peel in the ditch. I felt ashamed when I saw that. I couldn't really judge whoever had been there, because I was there too, just as curious, when I had no reason to be. I didn't know why I had come but, as I stood there, I began searching, my eyes panning over the grass like the camera in a murder film, looking for spots of blood, or the killer's cigarette butt, or a shred of torn clothing. There was something about the place that reminded me of the fossil room in the museum: I knew something had happened there, but only the faintest traces remained, more atmosphere than anything, like the fact of spines and flattened ribs embedded in the museum exhibits. I was pure attention, but I knew I was missing something, some clue that was waiting to be found. All that was needed was a shift in my awareness, like the shift of the dial on the radio that moved the frequency from a blur of noise and interference to a clear voice coming through on the air. I was listening too, but all I could hear was the wind in the poplar trees, twenty yards along the road. I don't know what I was listening for, maybe the dead girl's soul, bleeding away through the grass, seeping into the earth, as subtle and fleeting as melting snow.

The following Saturday, I waited near the fence, but I didn't see Bill or Mrs McCabe. Mum said they had probably gone visiting but I told her the car was still there. She just looked at me and laughed, then she said I shouldn't go making a big mystery out of everything.

'Run down to Brewster's for me,' she said. 'That'll give you something to do.'

The third disappearance was in the paper. It just said that a young girl had gone missing from home, and there were fears for her safety. Over the next few days, a massive search was in operation, but some time passed before the body was found.

After that, things changed. You could see it in people's faces: they had begun to suspect everybody, even their oldest neighbours. They felt betrayed; there was nothing that couldn't be made to look sinister, nothing that wasn't subject to interpretation. Worst of all, they could see in each other's faces that they were waiting for it to happen again. Now it was only a matter of time. People were powerless.

As it happened, the third victim was also the last. Her name was Cheryl Aldrich: she was three years below me at school, which also made her the youngest one to be taken. They found her in a derelict house about five miles from town; the body was lodged in the chimney, naked, but wrapped in old papers and rags, and held in place with a stick. She was the first victim the killer had bothered to hide. People were saying he'd kept her a prisoner for at least two days – there were cuts and burns all over her body and several fingers were broken. Whoever it was did other things too. I never found out what, but I knew it was sexual.

Now people were talking about the killer, they were all calling him the Man, with a capital M – it made him sound powerful and immutable, like the Lone Ranger or the Holy Roman Emperor. The children stopped saying they would be able to tell him a mile off, they just talked about Cheryl and said, no matter how careful you were, the Man could always get you if he wanted. We were only repeating what we'd heard, but it appealed to the morbid side of our characters, to know there were no certainties in life. Our parents couldn't protect us. Cheryl had gone to the shops in broad daylight to fetch a packet of Daz for her mum. The shops were only two hundred yards from where she lived; she had made it there but she hadn't come home. They had found the Daz on the waste ground near her house. Some parents started keeping their children away from school after that. I had to give up my paper round, but when I told Mr Brewster, he wasn't annoyed, he just nodded and said he was grateful I'd kept going for so long.

The Saturday after Cheryl was found, I went looking for Bill. I hadn't seen him for a while, and I'd started to wonder if I'd said something to offend him. I knocked at the back door several times. I could hear music but nobody answered. I knocked louder. At last Mrs McCabe came and opened the door a few inches.

'Hello, Paul,' she said. 'I'm sorry but Bill's sick. Can you come back another time?'

I could tell it wasn't true, not just because the music was playing, but from the look on her face.

'What's wrong with him?' I said.

She shook her head.

'I'm not sure,' she replied. 'We'll have to wait and see what the doctor says.'

I didn't say anything. I couldn't pretend I believed her. She wasn't really making much of an effort to convince me, anyway.

'Come back next week,' she said. Then she added, kindly, but also to cover up the lie, 'We don't want you catching anything, do we?'

I shook my head. She smiled, to show she appreciated my understanding, then she closed the door and turned the key in the lock. I waited on the step for a moment, listening to the music. It was Charlie Parker playing 'Ornithology'.

Snow came early that year. It took us by surprise: thick and fast for minutes at a time, swirling around outside the classroom window, then slower, more hesitant, as if it had got lost. Sometimes it seemed to be falling upwards. We had to switch on all the lights at two in the afternoon and it was a magical feeling, sitting with our backs to the window, sneaking a look when the teacher wasn't watching, feeling it settle on the hedges and roads all around us, crisp and white and cold, becoming everything it touched.

The killings had stopped. Some people thought the Man had moved on and, as if to support this theory, a five-year-old girl had been found dead in a field a hundred miles to the south. We heard about it on the radio. There were no real similarities to our cases, but we believed what we needed to believe. People wanted to settle into their old routines – to feel they could let their children go to boys' club or guides after school, to sleep through the night and not wake up at three in the morning to go wandering around the house, checking the windows were shut, the doors locked, the gardens empty. Most of all, they wanted to believe they knew their own neighbours.

They didn't, though. Nobody knows anybody for sure – at least, that's what I thought when I heard about Bill McCabe. I hadn't been to his house for a long time, at first out of resentment at having been deceived, then later because I didn't know if I was welcome. I hadn't even seen him for weeks, then the news arrived that he was dead. My mother told me about it over breakfast one morning. At first people thought it was an accident, but then, when the facts came through, it turned out he'd killed himself. He'd parked his car on the dirt road in the woods, not far from where Cheryl was found, then he'd swallowed a lot of pills and whisky.

As soon as they heard this, people started jumping to conclusions. The little girl in the south was forgotten. Now they had a suspect: for them, the suicide was an admission of guilt and, though there was no evidence to support the idea, they began making connections, finding patterns of coincidences, dismissing facts that didn't fit in with the theory, drawing together those that did. I was stunned. All of a sudden, in a way he could never have imagined, I stopped taking things for granted, the way Bill said I did. I went round to look for Mrs McCabe to let her know I didn't believe what people were saying, but she didn't answer the door and I knew, as far as she was concerned, I was the same as everybody else. The McCabes had lived in our town for years. Their lives had been quiet, perhaps a little lonely. Now they were evil.

It turned out Bill's death had nothing to do with the murders. He had a secret, but it wasn't what people thought – he'd been going out with a girl called Amanda Thompson, who worked in accounts at Connell's. Amanda was half his age: not very pretty, redheaded, freckle-faced, thin. They had been meeting once or twice a week after work and driving out to the woods. They'd sit out there, talking, or just watching the trees darken around them, startled by every bird and passing car on the road twenty yards away, afraid and lonely together. A couple of months before Bill killed himself Amanda had said she wanted to stop seeing him. She told the police she couldn't take it any more; she wanted a life for herself.

After she said they were finished, Bill must have gone on driving out to the woods and sitting there on his own, with the engine running to keep warm. People noticed the car: one man said he saw Bill walking around in the woods the day before Cheryl was killed and that was enough to start the rumour that he was the killer. Nobody thought to ask why that man hadn't spoken up before, or what he'd been doing out there in the woods. Even when Amanda came forward, there were people who said it only showed Bill wasn't the person everybody thought he was, if he could be having an affair with a girl half his age. Some people said Amanda was lucky to be alive.

Mrs McCabe stayed on for a while after Bill died. A few people were kind, but even they were suspicious. It was easy to see that she was in trouble and nobody could do very much to help. In her mind, the solid road she had been travelling for years had suddenly disappeared. Now she had nothing she could trust; she had stumbled on into loose scree and the ground kept shifting beneath her, a single thought became a landslide, and for desperate moments she had to work to keep her balance. I'd see her in the garden, walking around in the snow, looking at the ground as if she'd lost something. I wanted to help her but I didn't know how.

Around that time my mother had an argument with Cousin Madeleine. Maddy had said she'd be careful who she married and maybe she would live with the man first and get to know him.

'Don't be stupid, Madeleine,' my mother had said sharply, and Maddy had stared at her in amazement. I was surprised too: Madeleine was my mother's favourite niece, and she was always making a fuss of her. Usually, in my mother's eyes, Maddy could do no wrong.

'Well, look at Mrs McCabe,' Maddy had said. 'Who would have thought Bill McCabe would turn out like that?'

My mother gave her that look of hers that I knew meant not to talk about it in front of me, and Maddy shut up. Mum sent me out to the shops then and, when I got back, Maddy was gone. I don't know what happened after I left, but Mum was very pale, and Maddy didn't come round for quite a while after that. When she did, it was to tell us about her engagement to a man she'd met at work. My mother wanted to know all about him: she looked a bit disappointed when it turned out he was someone she'd never heard of, a man who had just moved to Weldon, to start a new job at Connell's. Still, they forgot their argument immediately; they just sat down at the table as if Maddy had never been away. I didn't understand them. It was a whole lot of fuss over nothing.

One Saturday afternoon, as it was just getting dark, I went out into the yard to fetch some coal. I didn't see Mrs McCabe at first. She was standing near the fence, just outside her back door; perhaps she had been there a while: she looked cold and lost, and I even thought for a moment she'd forgotten her key and couldn't get in.

I walked up to the fence and called out to her softly.

'Are you all right, Mrs McCabe?'

She looked at me and shook her head.

'I don't know what I'm going to do,' she said.

I thought she was going to cry. I didn't know what to say to make her feel better; but then, her face brightened, as if she'd just thought of something.

'Wait,' she said.

She went into the house and switched on the lights, leaving the door wide open. It was cold, but I waited; I could hear her moving around inside, but I couldn't work out what she was doing.

When she reappeared she was holding a large cardboard box full of records. I knew immediately what they were. I could see John Coltrane's face on the top of the pile.

'These are for you,' she said.

She held out the box and I took it, caught it really, because I think she would have let it fall if I hadn't.

'I've got no use for them,' she said. 'So you might as well

have them.' She almost sounded angry, but I wasn't sure if she was angry with me, or Bill, or someone else.

I began to thank her but, before I could say any more, she turned and started back towards the house. I noticed then she was wearing slippers.

'Say hello to your mother for me,' she said, as she closed the door behind her.

A week later, she moved. A man came in a blue car and drove right up the path to her front door. He helped her load some boxes into the boot, then they drove away. I was standing in the garden, watching; when they drove by, I waved, but I don't think she saw me. She had her head down and I think she was crying. I wondered if she was crying for Bill, or for the garden she was leaving behind, or for something else entirely.

I never saw her again. The man came a few more times; Mum said he was Mrs McCabe's brother. He organised everything: the removal men, the house sale. He even came one day and dug up some of the roses and shrubs; he wrapped them in newspapers and old sacking, then put them on the back seat of the car. Some of the plants were in flower and it looked odd as he drove away: a home-made funeral of old papers and muddy leaves, and a box of tools where the body might have been.

I still have the records. I keep them as they were given to me, in the cardboard box; somewhere in the back of my mind, I think of them as a loan, and I take better care of them than I would do if I'd bought them myself. They are arranged in alphabetical order: I take them out and play them sometimes, sitting in the front room, drinking coffee, watching the snow, or the rain, or the sunlight creeping across the gardens on Saturday mornings. There are forty-two records in all: John Coltrane, Miles Davis, Dizzy Gillespie, Charles Mingus, Thelonious Monk, Charlie Parker, Bud Powell, Lester Young.

I play them in sequence, starting at one end of the box then working my way through to the other. I don't mark my place: I trust myself to remember where I am. There are some I like more than others, but I never break the sequence and I don't play the same record twice. I've been playing them for years; I never let anybody else listen, though people sometimes see them among my things and ask. My answer is always the same: I'm keeping them for a friend. They're for me, and the McCabes, and the others who aren't here any more.

GRACELAND

You'd remember Wendy if you saw her. She was one of the daughters in *The Best Years of Your Life*, the one with the short black bob who dressed like a boy and was always getting into trouble. I imagine the show is still running somewhere, on some cable channel in the middle of the afternoon, and Wendy is still coming home, the twenty-five-year-old who's supposed to be somewhere between twelve and fifteen, pretty and confident and self-contained in a way that leaves her immune to everything. She was the one who played tricks on people, putting frogs in the bath, or spreading trails of trick blood across the floor. Whatever she did, she got away with it, and because she was on television, I was never altogether convinced that she was real – or at least, real in the ordinary sense, the way my mother was, or Miss Chandler, who lived next door, and taught English at my school. Maybe that was why I had a crush on her, when I was the age she was supposed to be in the programme. Naturally I never expected us to meet – we lived in such different dimensions. I certainly never thought she would find me by the side of a country road, where I'd been dumped by a lorry driver who'd picked me up two streets from home then decided he didn't like the sound of my voice. Or maybe he thought it would be better to have nothing to do with me, after I told him I was running away. I had run away five or six times in as many months, and each time I'd got a little further. If I hadn't met Wendy, I probably would have made it altogether that July afternoon, and who knows where I would be now.

It was a shock, seeing her. It was the kind of afternoon where anything can happen: a faint haze hung over the fields after the long warmth of the day, and I felt as if I was the last person in the world, standing alone on the lush verge, between an orchard and a wheat field. I had been there for around half an hour when the open-top car pulled up, and this beautiful woman asked me with a smile where I was going. I once fell through the ice on Bircomb Pond, and the shock was just like that, my whole body gloved in cold, my head emptying, an almost electrical sensation in the very marrow of my bones. If someone had told me, a few minutes before, that I would meet Wendy, I would have resolved to play it cool, and I probably would have managed a neutrality of sorts, the kind of gruff, awkward self-containedness that I usually assumed in such circumstances. As it was, my whole system was confounded. I had resolved, in the long half-hour before she arrived, that I wouldn't say anything about my plans to the next driver: I wouldn't be running away from home, I'd be headed for London, where my older brother was at college. Or my sister, maybe – that might sound better. I wouldn't say anything about Graceland, either: that only made people feel uncomfortable. As it was, though, I couldn't say a thing: I just stood there, in the afternoon heat, and stared at her till she laughed quietly, and told me to hop in. It was odd, that, when she said it, as if she were still the Wendy from the old days, in her white jeans and that black and white striped T-shirt, too young to drive, really, but capable of anything, and bound to get away with it, because that was how it had to be, for someone like her.

★　　★　　★

Looking back, I see that any story I might have told her would have made no impression whatsoever. It wasn't just that she would have seen right through me, standing by the road, so obviously fifteen in my cheap nylon jacket and faded jeans. Everybody I'd ever hitched a lift from had seen through me, whether I'd told them I was on the run from home or not, but most of them still gave me a lift, and only one had ever dumped me at the roadside and told me to go back to my parents. It might have made a difference if I'd told her about Graceland, but I doubt it. Looking back, I see now that she really did think of me as someone her own age: that was why she had stopped. I have to work hard to see her as she really looked that day – most of the time, I imagine her as she was on television, suspended in that magical light where, if you have the gift, you can be anyone you want to be – but with some effort I remember that she looked about thirty, and I can still see the wrinkles around her mouth and eyes, which would have been barely noticeable, if she hadn't been wearing so much make-up. It made me think of my mother, who always did that on the odd occasions when Dad took her out: she would sit down at the mirror as a forty-year-old woman and rise, about an hour later, looking ten years older. Still, magic has a long, possibly infinite, half-life, and the only thing that really mattered was that *this woman* was Wendy. Even when I saw her as she was, I still saw her as she could be, as television, and the attention of millions, had made her.

She seemed happy, and I let myself imagine that she was glad to have met me on the road, that there was some instant bond between us that cancelled out any difference in age or status. She did most of the talking, to begin with, but she didn't introduce herself, or say anything about television, or the show. I suppose you get to be that way, once you've been famous. You don't talk about yourself, you show an interest in the other person – and that was what she did. She wanted to know where I lived and where I was going and, when I'd dutifully stumbled through my older brother story, she asked if I went to London often. When I said I did, she wanted to know about my favourite places. The car sped along the country road, while I did some hard thinking.

'I like the National Gallery,' I said, at last.

Wendy laughed. It obviously wasn't the answer she'd been expecting.

'Really?' She sounded incredulous. 'What else?'

'I went to Madame Tussaud's once,' I said. 'That was pretty interesting.'

As soon as the car had pulled up, I had wanted to tell her my idea about Graceland, and how I'd started thinking about it when I saw the waxwork of Elvis at Madame Tussaud's, and then, a few weeks later, a picture of the house, looking much smaller than I had expected, in one of my mother's magazines. I thought she would like the idea, the fact that Graceland didn't have to be in one place or another, how it existed in people's minds, and everyone could have a Graceland, if they wanted. Maybe that house in *The Best Years of Your Life* had been Graceland for some people: it was just an idea of what you most desired, of the magical, of everything you didn't have, all the places and moments you had missed, through no fault of your own. I wanted to tell her that – because it would have been a way of telling her something else – but I couldn't: as soon as I mentioned Madame Tussaud's she laughed again, and I was too embarrassed.

'Sorry,' she said. 'I didn't mean to laugh at you. Actually, I like Madame Tussaud's too. I go there quite a lot.'

I didn't believe her, but I was glad she was making the effort to be nice and, after that, the conversation was a little easier. I began to relax, and now it was my turn to do most of the talking. I didn't tell her about running away, though, and before I could say anything about Graceland, she interrupted.

'Listen,' she said. 'I'm not going all the way to London. Well, not right away. But I'll be going there later. There's just one thing I have to do first.'

She paused and glanced over at me, as if she expected some reaction, so I nodded.

'I have to drop in and see some friends,' she continued. 'It's a bit of a party, in fact, and I just want to say hello. You can come too, if you like – and then we'll go on to London. I'll drop you off at your brother's. What do you think?'

She didn't look at me this time. She kept her eyes on the road, with that air of someone who expects to be looked at, and doesn't want to wait too obviously for a reply.

'That'd be great,' I said.

'Sure?'

'Definitely.'

'Your brother won't mind? If we're a bit late, say?'

'No,' I said, quickly. I almost added that he was a big fan of hers, but then I remembered that I didn't have a brother and, besides, I suddenly realised that I wasn't supposed to know who she was. It wasn't just good manners on her part that had made her ask about me and say nothing about herself. For some reason, she wanted to forget about *The Best Years of Your Life*, and I wasn't going to be the one to remind her.

We got to the house around eight o'clock. The first thing I noticed was the sign on the gate, which was standing wide-open, and Wendy drove in quickly, straight past the trees at the entrance-way and along the drive, but I still caught a glimpse of the black and white lettering in the half-light among the shrubs. *Graceland.* It startled me for a moment; then the house appeared, much larger than I had expected, and lit up from end to end with brightly coloured lights.

'Is this it?' I asked.

Wendy nodded. I looked at her face and noticed that, as she parked the car and unlocked the door on her side, she looked a little nervous. Then, with a surreptitious flutter, she opened her bag and, under cover of powdering her nose, slipped something out of a cellophane wrapper and into her mouth. She swallowed carefully.

'There,' she said.

I looked away. The big main door at the front of the house was closed, but there was another to one side of the car park, a set of old-fashioned French doors that someone had left open, with a big bunch of balloons pinned to the lintel. As I opened my door, a girl of around sixteen, in a bright-red ballerina's dress, ran out squealing, followed by a much older man dressed as a clown. Wendy watched them disappear into the garden.

'Looks like fancy-dress,' she said.

I glanced at her.

'Didn't you know?'

'No,' she said. 'There are parties here all the time. I can't keep track of them.'

She crossed the car park to the French doors, her feet crunching on the gravel.

'Come on,' she called. 'Let's get a drink.'

Inside, there were at least forty, maybe fifty people, all standing in one huge glass-roofed space, lit here and there with candles and fairy-lights. They were all in fancy-dress. The nearest group – a harlequin, a fairy, another clown and a man in a red devil suit – turned to look at us as we came in, but they didn't seem to recognise Wendy and they quickly went back to their conversation. Further on, a whole gang of fairies was standing by a long table covered with drinks and food, talking loudly and laughing; some were even waving sparklers around. Wendy stopped just inside the doorway and looked into the crowd. I wasn't sure if she was looking for somebody in particular, or just pretending to look, and I had begun to feel nervous, what with the party being fancy-dress, and her not seeming to know about it. I was relieved when a tall, thick-set man with slicked-back hair and a white suit stepped up out of the crowd – though it took me a few moments to realise who he was supposed to be.

'Wendy!' he called loudly, taking her by the arm. Wendy flinched, almost imperceptibly. 'What a surprise!'

He glanced at me, then turned back to her.

'Who's your little friend?' he asked in the same loud, mock-friendly voice.

'He's on his way to London,' Wendy said, quietly. 'I'm giving him a lift.'

The man laughed.

'Really,' he said. 'Well, bring him over and we'll see if we can't corrupt him.' Then he leaned down into Wendy's face and murmured, 'Or are we too late for that – ' before resuming in the loud, party voice, with just a hint of Elvis twang, 'What's your poison, son?'

He led the way to the table and the fairies dispersed in a flurry of laughter and sparklers. Wendy picked up a glass of red wine, and the man in the Elvis suit waved his hand generously over the massed bottles and glasses.

'Help yourself,' he said. He turned back to Wendy and assumed his quiet voice.

'Stewart isn't here,' he said.

I kept glancing at the table. I couldn't decide what to have, but I didn't want them to think I was listening. Not that I could avoid it. They weren't making any effort to keep their conversation from me.

'Really?' Wendy smiled softly. 'I suspect he'll be here, though. Eventually.'

Elvis grinned. Looking at him then, the thought came to me that I had never seen anyone who looked less like the King.

'Well, sure, honey,' he said. 'You know Stewart. Just promise me – I don't want any fuss. You remember what happened last time.'

Wendy nodded.

'I just want a word,' she said, handing me a glass of wine. 'Then we'll be on our way.'

Elvis grinned, but he didn't say anything. He just kept his eyes fixed on Wendy a moment longer, then turned to me.

'Enjoy yourself,' he said, making it sound like a warning. Before either of us could say anything more, he turned and walked off into the crowd, and I heard his big, party voice behind us, greeting another gang of arrivals. Wendy looked round eagerly, then turned back to me.

'Come on,' she said, grabbing a bottle of red wine and a couple of fresh glasses. 'Let's get some air.'

It was much cooler, now. The air was fresh, with a slight breeze blowing across a perfectly manicured lawn, to where Wendy had sat us down, in two old-fashioned wooden deck-chairs on the patio. It felt oddly criminal to me, to be sitting there, enjoying a stranger's wine, in a garden he must have taken a great deal of care over – especially when the stranger was someone who obviously disliked our presence in his home. Wendy didn't seem to mind, though; all of a sudden, she was bright and happy again, confident and invulnerable, the way she had always been on television. I suppose that was what I most liked about her, in *The Best Years*: no matter what happened, even when she was in trouble, she looked at home wherever she was, as if she could always tell that things would work out in the end. That's probably the real art in that kind of acting: where other characters would mug it up, looking worried and anxious, or trying to make the audience think there was some kind of danger, Wendy never took anything seriously, she just kept on being Wendy. That was the reason we loved her. Now, suddenly, in the half-light, I could see that Wendy again, and I was happy.

I've wondered, sometimes, what it means to be happy. I used to think it was a state of being, a semi-permanent condition, and I suppose I felt cheated because I didn't have what other people call a happy childhood, or a happy home, or any of the big, happy occasions in my life that people always take such trouble to record. Yet, if I stop and think, I know I have been happy, in an odd, detached way, for moments or even hours at a time. I wasn't leaping up and down, or going around singing – it wasn't that kind of happiness, the kind you see on television, *happy* in the way Wendy's sister Grace always was, because she was pretty, and popular in school, and always had something to do. My happy times have been so quiet as to be almost imperceptible. They usually came when I was alone, walking by the side of a road, or sitting under a tree between rides. Sometimes, when I was running away from home, I would think of myself as being on the road, just travelling, always between places, like the men in the old country songs. I would have stopped somewhere, and it would feel as if time had stopped all around me, as if the whole world of other people had moved off somewhere – just a few feet from where I was standing, maybe, so I could still see and hear it, but it was muffled and removed, so that it didn't matter any more. There would be a happiness, then, which I couldn't really describe: all I can say is, it was a kind of detachment, a settled feeling, a new rhythm in the world that included me. It was simply a matter of stopping, of being wholly physical and isolate, sitting in the sun and letting the warmth seep into my skin, or realising I was thirsty and going into a corner shop to buy a cold drink. Sometimes I could be happy beyond belief just from sitting down by the side of a country road and feeling the wind on my face.

We must have sat out there for an hour or more, drinking the wine, listening to the music in the background, and the occasional soft flutter of birds in the shrubbery. I wasn't used to wine, and I hadn't eaten much that day, but I didn't think I was drunk. Now and then, a couple in fancy-dress would erupt noisily around the corner of the house, catch sight of us, then disappear into the garden and, once, the door behind us opened, hung ajar for a moment or so, then closed quietly before I could see who it was. After a while, the wine ran out, and Wendy said she was going to get another bottle. She stood over me, smiling, as she said it, and I remember how she looked then: fifteen years old, in her black and white T-shirt, with the blue from the garden lamp on her face.

I waited a long time. For a while, I didn't even notice that she had been gone too long. My body felt loose and warm, like something new that I had just found, something well-tuned and easy to use. I thought about Graceland again, about how visitors always expected it to be much larger than it was. They would travel from all over the world to stand outside and gaze at the house, and they would come away every time with a sense of wanting more, with that same sense of frustration you get when you hear a story and you don't understand it. Somebody should have told them that they had come to the wrong place, that they should have gone on living with just the word, and the house they imagined, because everyone had a different Graceland, and it wasn't fair on Elvis, to try to steal his dreams. My mind was wandering, I suppose, and I don't actually remember falling asleep. I only recall the moment of fright and cold, when I started awake, thinking I'd heard Wendy's voice, her fifteen-year-old's voice from *The Best Years*, calling to me for help.

Inside, the glass-roofed space was empty. Most of the candles had burnt out, and the room was almost dark. There was litter everywhere – empty bottles, streamers, dead sparklers and cigarette butts, scattered across the floor – and the air smelled of stale smoke and spilt wine. I had expected to see Wendy, but there was no one there and, in a moment of panic, I thought she might have left without me. I was about to rush out, to find the car, when the voice came again, a soft, hurt cry from the far end of the glass-covered room. I started across the floor, then, towards the narrow doorway I could only just see beyond the shadows. I was almost halfway when I realised that I wasn't alone after all. A man in a light-coloured suit was sitting off to one side, smoking a cigarette. It was only when he spoke that I realised who he was.

'Where do you think *you're* going?' he said.

I stopped dead. The man stood slowly and moved out of the shadows. It was the same man who had greeted us when we arrived, and he was wearing the same white suit, but now his face was covered with a full-size Elvis mask.

'Oh,' he said. 'It's you.' He came a few steps closer.

'Don't you know, sonny,' he said, in the Elvis drawl, 'that this is way past your bedtime?'

Before I could say anything, the voice came again from the room behind him – a sharp cry this time, a cry of sudden and unnecessary pain. Involuntarily, I moved towards the door, but my muscles felt slack, all of a sudden, and I felt I would lose control of my body entirely and fall in a heap on the floor, or jerk away, like a puppet on strings. In the pit of my stomach I felt a sickening lightness, as if any centre of gravity I had ever had was dissolving. For his part, Elvis moved as easily and deliberately as before, unhurriedly blocking my way, so I stopped dead in my tracks again, frozen with indecision and fear. Beyond him, the room fell silent again, which frightened me as much, or even more than the cry I had heard a moment before.

Elvis stood in my path, watching me, waiting to see what I would do next. He made it obvious that, no matter what I did, he was more than capable of handling it – and that was when I knew I would do nothing. Even if Wendy began to scream blue murder, or cry for help, I was incapable of passing the masked figure who stood between us. At the same time, I understood that *he* knew I was helpless. There was something in the way his body relaxed, in the sense I had that he was smiling behind the mask, smiling softly with triumph and contempt, there was something in his whole ease of being that inscribed helplessness into my very soul. And now, when there was no need, when he knew for sure that I was incapable of action, he stepped forward. He moved slowly and, if I had run, he probably would have made no effort to pursue me. Yet I couldn't run. Some remnant of pride held me there, I suppose, or perhaps it was just the shame I felt, at abandoning Wendy, or at my own helplessness. Even now, I feel a swell of anger when I think that I did nothing, even to protect myself. When he moved closer I could smell the cigarettes on his breath, and the sheer bulk of his man's body was like a gravity field, pulling me into his orbit. He reached out slowly; then, with a quick, easy movement, he took hold of my neck and raised his cigarette to my face.

'I don't like you, sonny.' He spoke slowly, in the same Elvis drawl. 'I don't like people who come where they're not wanted. I don't like people who drink other people's drinks and poke their noses into other people's business.'

All the while, he was tightening his grip, with a sickening, measured power. At the same time, the cigarette ember moved closer, till I felt it against my cheek. My mind blanked. I have no idea, to this day, how far he intended to go, but at the time, I knew there were no limits to the pleasure he would take in damaging me. I didn't even see the ballerina – she was standing behind me, I suppose – but when she called out, Elvis loosened his grip and let me fall. I felt sick and giddy, but there was something in my mind, now that it was too late, that found its bearings and got me out of there. I lay still a moment; I could hear the woman's voice, from an impossible distance, asking him what was going on, then I heard Elvis move away. I think he was trying to reassure her, to get her to go back to bed, and if she had given in sooner, he might have returned to me, to finish what he'd started. As it was, she kept talking and, though I couldn't hear what it was she was saying to him, I knew she was trying to help me. The delay gave me the chance to escape, but it was nothing but complete and utter panic that got me to my feet and out of there, staggering to the door and then running, while his laughter rang out behind me, through the still house.

I ran as far as the gate, then along the road in the dark, away from the house, stumbling as I went, but too scared to stop. It was a long time before I slowed down – from fatigue, rather than the understanding that I was out of danger, that no one was coming after me. I had no idea where I was. I stopped and looked around: it was an ordinary country road, among fields; I could see a pale orange glow on the sky, some distance away, but no sign of traffic, or other houses. Nearby, some animals were standing together by a fence; a dim, ruminant presence in the summer darkness. I hadn't paid much attention to the road on the way to the party; now, I saw that my only option was to keep walking till I came to a main road and found out where I was.

I must have gone three or four miles before I came to the lay-by. I kept thinking of Wendy, and wondering what had happened in that room, and I felt sick with shame, that I had done nothing to help her. At the same time, I was angry with her, too, for she must have known what could happen at the party and she should never have gone or, if she really had to go, she shouldn't have taken me with her. I remembered what Elvis had said, about me going where I wasn't wanted, and I told myself that everything was her fault.

Then I saw the lay-by. I had no idea what time it was, but it must have been late – after midnight, at least. The cars were parked side by side, with their headlights on full-beam – three of them, with a middle-aged couple in each, sitting upright in the front seats, gazing out at nothing. They were all around the same age: the men were dressed identically in dark-coloured suits; the women had their hair done up as if they were going out somewhere special and they were wearing print dresses, with thin crocheted cardigans over their shoulders. Two of the women wore glasses, the kind secretaries were always supposed to wear. I'm not sure when, or even if they saw me – if they did, they took no notice. They sat stock-still, their eyes fixed on some distant point. I turned around to see what they were looking at, but there was nothing except the white beam of their combined headlamps, reaching away into the darkness. I waited. I suppose I expected them to notice me, maybe even to help in some way, but they didn't move. After a while, I walked on. For a few miles more, I half-expected Wendy to appear, to drive up suddenly and apologise, and take me to London. She didn't, of course. Finally, I stopped walking and climbed over a stile into an empty field. I must have slept for some of the time, because I remember having dreams, though I have no idea what they were about. All I know is, when I came to myself again, there was something I had seen and forgotten, a clue that would have explained everything, nothing more than a detail, but something essential that was lodged in my mind for ever, even though I couldn't find it.

Eventually I made it all the way to London and, though it wasn't easy, with no money, and nowhere to stay, I managed to spin it out for almost a fortnight. Still, nothing lasts for long. My parents had called the police – just as they had done on all the other occasions I had run away – and by a series of accidents, and mistakes on my part, I was picked up and taken home. I never saw Wendy again. I haven't even seen her on television, though someone told me recently that there had been repeats. I was in hospital for a while, after that trip – I suppose the party had given me a bit of a fright – but eventually I wandered away and, though it's been almost twenty years, I still disappear, every now and then. Naturally, I haven't found Graceland yet. Once, as a holiday, I went to Memphis, like all those other pilgrims, just to see what it was like – but I knew it wasn't the place I was looking for. Sometimes I tell myself I should stop searching, that Graceland doesn't exist, except in the word itself and in my imagination. That's easy to say, of course, but it turns out that life is much longer than I had ever expected, and I have to do something, to stay occupied. Most of the time, I understand that, like the others, I'm probably looking in all the wrong places but, so far, all I know is that Memphis, or anywhere else, is an illusion. I've thought about it long enough to know, sitting up late in rented rooms and describing the journey to myself, looking out at dark gardens in the suburbs and imagining an endless highway of gas stations and cheap motels, and mile-deep woods just beyond the edges of the light. I know it's an illusion because I played that game every night in the hospital: every night I'd choose a place on the half-formed map of America that I carry in my head, from years of old B movies and rock and roll songs. It's probably there, somewhere, in Illinois, or Colorado: an ordinary house in the suburbs, with a neat lawn and a Coup de Ville in the drive. It's the kind of place where Wendy would live for ever, and it's probably as much as Elvis was really looking for – an idea of home, something in black and white, the smell of cheap lilac soap and the radio playing in the kitchen. Breakfast in the morning dusk and midnight feasts of beer and fudge cake with a girl like Wendy; and maybe, from time to time, as a kind of joke, a Hallowe'en night of horror films in a darkened room, and a mouthful of trick blood on the bathroom floor, to keep the night at bay.